T0065505

NIGHT WHISPERS OF
A PAINTED LADY

JODI EMBRY

WESTBOW
PRESS®
A DIVISION OF THOMAS NELSON
& ZONDERVAN

WestBow Press books may be ordered through booksellers or by contacting:

WestBow Press
A Division of Thomas Nelson & Zondervan
1663 Liberty Drive
Bloomington, IN 47403
www.westbowpress.com
844-714-3454

Scripture quotations are taken from the Holy Bible, New Living Translation,
copyright ©1996, 2004, 2015 by Tyndale House Foundation. Used by permission
of Tyndale House Publishers, Carol Stream, Illinois 60188. All rights reserved.

ISBN: 978-1-6642-6201-0 (sc)
ISBN: 978-1-6642-6203-4 (hc)
ISBN: 978-1-6642-6202-7 (e)

Library of Congress Control Number: 2022905724

Print information available on the last page.

WestBow Press rev. date: 05/05/2022

Softy I announce my presence with shimmering hues of memories and I tap gently on your awareness seeking to be heard. All those who live within my walls will be who I become. Relax while I speak to you in gentle whispers.

CONTENTS

DEDICATED TO
MY MOTHER

WHO ALWAYS SAID I SHOULD WRITE

Mom, I have fulfilled your wish with two published stories and multiple short stories. They have flowed from my heart onto paper. As I write I often think of you and wish you were here to enjoy them. I think you would be proud of my accomplishments. You have been my inspiration to share the feelings of my heart.

Thank you, Mom.

ACKNOWLEDGEMENTS

I have been blessed to have Lynn Terry as my friend and editor. She has faithfully labored through my mistakes, putting me back on track when I have gone off the rails.

Her valuable insights showed me a clearer presentation for my story. She introduced new ways to add vitality to my active scenes. I owe her a great debt of gratitude for all her labor of love editing my story. She asked nothing in return, only to see the story to its finish Thank you from the bottom of my heart, Lynn.

Jodi

THE DISCOVERY OF
THE PAINTED LADY

Tricia was driving around the Helena countryside looking for a new home for her and her husband, Tom. It wasn't a pressing crusade to find a new place in their immediate future; she just wanted to relocate from their rambling ranch home at their current location to a home with personality and history. It was on this Tuesday that she turned down Madison Street, an older part of town, when she spied an old Victorian two story home. She drove up to the driveway and observed the beauty of a wrap-around porch, a turret on the top of the second floor and the delicate faded trim. It was obviously in some state of disrepair and she knew in her heart that they would love this place. It had a FOR SALE sign in the front yard but had no agent listed. She jotted down the address, 812 Madison, and called her husband, Tom, who was a realtor.

He looked up the record of current ownership with the listed phone number for the residence. He headed home to share his findings with Tricia. The current owner was an elderly lady who needed to sell the home because she was no longer able to maintain it. Evidently her daughter insisted she sell the home place so she could move in with her. She hadn't listed with a realtor because she was secretly hoping that no one would notice that it was for sale; and by not listing with a realtor it would not be on the active market. She really didn't want to sell and leave the home that she had known and loved and where her three children were raised.

At Tricia's insistence Tom placed a call to the owner of the house and made an appointment to come by and see the home. The lady, Mrs. Opal Covington, was surprised to hear that someone was interested in buying her home. Arrangements were made to meet the next day at 1:00 in the afternoon to see the interior and for Tom to check the perimeter of the house and the grounds. Tricia was excited and felt that she had finally found her dream home.

When they arrived the next day, Mrs. Covington had prepared tea and a simple pound cake for them. She was a sweet and soft-spoken lady with bright eyes and a dimple in her wrinkled cheeks. They were ushered into the living room furnished with an old cherry wood sofa with worn upholstery. There were two chairs that showed years of wear, but were still sturdy. After they were seated, Mrs. Covington, or Opal as she chose to be called, began to tell a bit about the house.

MIKE AND OPAL COVINGTON

She and her husband, Mike, had moved into the house when they were first married and had raised their three children, Brenda, Alice, and George there. Her eyes began to mist as she recalled some of the special times in the home. Before the girls had gone off to college, they had many birthday parties, Halloween trick or treat encounters, and festive meals at Thanksgiving and Christmas. But the best memory was when the girls had sleep-overs. They stayed up all night giggling and talking about boys. Food and treats were always on hand when their friends came after school to study. George was always teasing the girls and playing tricks on them. There were bruises and bumps and even some frightening adventures as the children grew.

When they left home to attend college, the house became *whisper quiet*. As each one became engaged, they returned to have their weddings and reception parties at home. Opal's voice soften as she recalled, " We had such beautiful parties with festive decorations, flowers filling the entire house and special music floating throughout the entire house. Those were wonderful times!"

Within the walls of every house there are memories of love, fun, sorrow and excitement, and so it was with this regal home. Three generations had shared their lives within these walls and Tricia and Tom were now considering adding their life history to this grand Victorian lady.

Tom and Tricia were fascinated with Opal's recounting of life in this spacious home and with their encouragement she continued telling the long-ago stories of some of the history of her home when she was raising her family. She was quick to fondly recall how tight knit a family they were.

Her daughter, Brenda, after graduating from high school, left home to attend college. She received her teaching degree and moved to California for a teaching position. She married and had two children. Since they lived so far away Opal and her husband, Mike, seldom heard the laughter of their voices echoing through the house. "Oh, how we missed their kisses and hugs and the happy sound of games played in the back yard. But they, too, grew up and followed their calling to different careers", sighed Opal.

Tricia interrupted Opal's train of thought to question her about her husband.

"Oh, yes Mike was a mining engineer supervisor in Montana and was injured on the job as a young man of only forty-two. He was inspecting a silver mine deep in the bowels of the mineshafts when one of the supporting timbers, which had been compromised by blasting, collapsed. He was rushed to the hospital suffering three fractured ribs, a broken shoulder, and a severe concussion with a deep gash across the back of his head. He lingered on the edge of life or death for a week but then began to return from his coma and gradually started the long road of recovery. He was, however, never able to return to his job and became a partial invalid living at home. I don't think the pain ever completely left his body." There were tears in her soft blue eyes and the pain was still etched in her wrinkled face.

She quickly recovered from that memory and, apologizing for her tears, insisted that the two of them have another piece of cake and a fresh cup of tea.

Sensing Opal's pain regarding that period in her life, Tricia was eager to change the subject and asked if she could see the interior of the home. Opal described the layout of the first and second floors and told them to explore on their own since she was no longer able to climb the stairs.

Tricia's thoughts were spinning. The kitchen was large enough for a breakfast nook and an island for a modernized kitchen. There was a small closet and a screened in back porch leading to an overgrown back yard. There was a room for Tom's study and for her art projects on the first floor. There was a large dinning room and a spacious living room. What a perfect room for a family room, Tricia thought. Her excitement grew as she walked up the stairs to the second floor. There were five large bedrooms, two of which could be converted into a large master bedroom with a modern spa bath. One of the three smaller rooms could serve as a quite retreat area and the remaining two bedrooms would be guest bedrooms. Her imagination was running wild as she checked each room, the closets and windows. This was going to be such a joy converting this house into her dream home. Tom was busily checking the outside of the house for any needed major repairs and any obvious plumbing and heating problems.

Tom and Tricia made a tentative offer on the house. Opal was taken by surprise and reluctantly agreed to their terms. There would have to be a contract drawn up, an inspection done and arrangements at the bank for a loan. This would take a week or so. Upon leaving both parties were awash with the speedy commitment they had made. They needed time to settle their minds on this new future.

After they, left Opal sat down trying to digest what had just happened to her and her home. She called her daughter in California with the news. As soon as Brenda answered the phone she was aware from her mother's trembling voice that something traumatic had just happened.

"Brenda, a couple have just left the house and have offered to purchase our home for the agreed price. I am feeling so sad thinking of leaving our home to strangers. All our lives are intertwined with the memories that linger here within these walls. They were a lovely couple and I am sure that they will enjoy this place as much as our family did. No doubt they will bring it to life again, but it feels like I am burying what is left of my life as I release the house to strangers." At this she began crying and seemed unable to stop and take control of her emotions.

Brenda wanted to reach out and comfort her mom reassuring her that she had done the right thing. She yearned to reach through the phone and hug her tightly. She had thoughts of happy times running with her sister and brother in the backyard, playing hide-and-seek in the big rooms and closets in the attic where her dad had created a playhouse. Memories of all the holiday meals, the birthday parties, the celebrations of high school and college graduation, and her wedding reception opened a floodgate of memories. They seemed to engulf her. She swallowed hard and, regaining her composure, said, "Mom, I will fly up and stay with you while we sort out all the details. Meanwhile I will begin making a cozy little apartment in our home for you. You will have your independence and yet be close for us to visit. We will go shopping, have special lunches together and sit on the patio reliving the wonderful memories that are ours from long ago."

Opal lingered before replying as she dabbed the tears from her eyes finally saying, "Yes, that would be fine and I will look forward to spending time together again. Let me know when you will be coming and I will have your old room ready. I can hardly wait for you to come."

The next day Tom took his break time from work to go to the courthouse to search for the original information about the house they were going to buy. He especially wanted to know the architect and what the plans revealed about the plumbing, electrical wiring and the exact measurements of the lot. After some intense searching and digging through old records he finally found the name of the original architect and builder. The Queen Anne style was adorned with gingerbread woodwork and colorful exterior. Tom became more and more impressed with the quality and workmanship that was apparent from the original plans. As he read further, he discovered the original owner, S. L. Humphreys, was a wealthy banker from New York City who built the house for his wife. The original marble steps were still there, as was the stained glass window in the front door. The original exterior colors were faded but still recognizable. Tom was eager to get home and share all this information about the house and the Humphreys family history.

BIRTH OF A PAINTD
LADY IN MONTANA

Mr. Humphreys stood out above all the other men in Helena's early history. Looking further into the family records, Tricia and Tom later discovered the Humphreys enjoyed many happy times as well as times clouded with sorrow and sadness. Tricia would experience a taste of their sadness in the weeks to come. She would have an eerie awareness of a mother's grief over her dying son.

SAMUEL AND BEATRICE HUMPHREYS

S. L. Humphreys, known by his friends as Samuel, was a successful banker in New York City. He met beautiful young Beatrice Nolan at a dinner party hosted by his bank's owner. Beatrice was born into a wealthy family, receiving the best education at prodigious schools. She moved with ease in society circles and was a member of the fine arts community.

Samuel fell in love with the vivacious young woman the first time he saw her. They had courted for a year when Samuel sought her father's permission for her hand in marriage. Following a beautiful wedding they lived in a stately home in an affluent section of the city. Their lifestyle was one of beautiful things and gatherings with Samuel's rich and famous friends.

Two years later their son, Christopher was born. He was the joy of their lives. Even with a young son their life continued in a predictable routine. They remained active in social circles, entertaining friends and business associates in their home. When Christopher was five years old, Beatrice became pregnant with her second child.

Samuel continued to rise to higher positions within the bank, and yet as he did so he became restless and discontented with his professional life. The idea of leaving New York City took shape and he became obsessed with the challenge of moving to a frontier territory. He wanted to make a difference and this seemed to be the right direction to do so. He intensified his research regarding the Montana Territory, noting that the gold rush in Helena was creating enormous wealth. There was an opportunity to establish a new bank!

He was unsure how Beatrice would react to his idea, so he put off discussing it with her until one evening as they lingered over dinner. As carefully as he, could he explained his feelings and the desire to move to a more challenging life. Beatrice was horrified at the thought of leaving her beautiful home. How could she live without the luxuries she was accustomed to? The thought of being separated from her parents was unthinkable! Samuel gently tried to console her, reassuring her that he would provide for her and Christopher and the new baby. But she would have none of it.

Screaming, she fled to the bedroom and flung herself onto the bed. Between sobs she cried, "Christopher is only five years old and too young to be uprooted from all he has known." Samuel tried to console her as best he could. He gathered her into his arms reassuring her nothing would be decided now. The topic set aside for two years.

When Elliot, a healthy robust boy turned two, Samuel thought it might be time to discuss the topic of relocating. This time Beatrice was not as emotional about the idea as before. They explored everything involved with the move to the Montana Territory. Beatrice began making a mental list of her own. They reached an agreement deciding what to leave and what to take with them. Above all they were satisfied that both boys were physically able to make the arduous journey.

After arriving in Montana, they found a modest home near the building site for Samuel's bank. Even though time healed some of Beatrice's anxieties about relocating, she still missed the life she had in New York City. Although she longed for the music and the cultural advantages of home, she was far too busy now and had little time for mulling over these losses. It seemed that all she did was attend to the needs of her two young sons, plus there was the endless cooking, continuous laundry, and all without any domestic help. This left her exhausted and moody at the end of the day. As time wore on, she sought something she enjoyed. She threw herself into planting vegetable and flower gardens. This brought some brightness and sense of accomplishment into her life.

Samuel proved himself, within a year, to be a successful investor and banker. As the town grew and money freely flowed, Samuel once again gained wealth and popularity. Now he could afford a beautiful home for Beatrice and his sons.

Several large mansions were built on the outskirts of Helena. Samuel purchased a sizeable property at 802 Madison Street. He hired an architect to build a stately Queen Anne Victorian house for his wife. The design included ornate and elaborate woodwork etched in gold throughout the interior. The exterior included elegant balconies with spindle railings. Samuel also insisted that there be gingerbread design around the front of the house and on the turret. Samuel hoped this beautiful home would replace the one that Beatrice once had enjoyed. He designed a name plaque painted pale pink with two beautiful carved red roses at each end. Using his pet name for his wife, BEA, he had QUEEN BEA carved and etched in gold placed above the front entrance. It would greet all who entered their home as a testimony of his love and adoration for Beatrice. The architect suggested gray, plum, rose, bone and navy blue for the exterior colors. The elegant new house was the perfect picture of grandeur, a palace for his queen.

Beatrice moved into her new home determined to bring it up to the elegance of her former beloved home. She was confident her lifestyle would be restored. The family settled in and for a while, the atmosphere was magical.

Little Elliot became seriously ill with pneumonia and his lungs were horribly congested. For weeks his lungs were unable to rid the horrible congestion Even after his fever broke, he remained weak and listless. During those painful laborious breathing difficulties Beatrice held him close to her heart as she softly sang lullabies. Her heart was broken and many nights Samuel heard her crying as she whispered her love to Elliot. Her tearful prayers rose like vapors, seeping into the crevices and nooks of the spacious room. The night whisperings had begun within the Painted Lady.

Two months later Elliot was gaining strength but not fully

recovered. Beatrice was concerned he might not grow into a strong healthy lad and maybe it would affect him into adulthood. This concern haunted her and she sank deeper into depression. She brooded as dark shadows flooded the landscape of her mind. The only solution she saw was to take her boys back for a time to her parents in New York City. She reasoned that Elliot could receive better medical attention for his weakened condition. She and Samuel discussed this idea and came to an agreement that a visit to Beatrice's parents would be best, especially for the medical help that Elliot needed.

One week later on an overcast February morning, Beatrice and the boys boarded a train that would take them far away from their father. Tears flowed freely as each child was hugged and kissed. Beatrice clung to Samuel, reluctant to release her grasp, fearing that this could be the last time she would feel his strong arms around her. As brave as Samuel was, he too, felt stinging tears coursing down his cheeks. He did not know how he could continue his daily life without them.

Gold was the driving source of wealth when Montana was a Territory. Last Chance Gulch Mine, was a location that produced both gold and silver. The discovery made the men seeking their treasure into thieves, robbers, and yet many trustworthy individuals became solid citizens who built churches and schools. The U.S. Army had a basecamp for the purpose of maintaining order and keeping the transport of gold safe. They also had the responsibility of protecting the residents from the Indians. They had a camel division, which Tom thought was amusing. Many Chinese men began to fill the mining camps as well as settlers from back east and from other countries. Because there wasn't much agriculture to provide fresh produce, food was shipped in by wagon or stagecoach. The price of flour was $1.00 a pound and a good-sized cabbage cost $10. Most of the people living there were rich with gold and were willing to pay the price. However, as the population increased and settled in Helena, many families began raising their own vegetables. Meat was supplied with the arrival of a cattle drive into Montana Territory which in turn, supplemented the abundant wildlife that was native to the area. Tom was most interested to learn that men of wealth gave generously to the establishment of churches, schools and theatres.

Helena, at this time was a bustling town with many churches as well as many saloons. A grade school, hotels, grocery stores, a bank, and an opera house were quickly built in the very early days. Railroad lines were built and heavy-laden freight trains brought supplies to town, replacing the slow delivery by pack mules. The trains also brought passengers to the area. In 1888 Helena became the railroad center of Montana, changing the history of a frontier town to one bustling with activity.

Tom thought Tricia would be interested in learning that women of the Woman Suffrage Movement had several leaders in Helena. They held meetings to appeal for the right of women to vote, sending their request to the Governor's office. There was great support from the public, including the men, and received little or no resistance from the public for this to become law.

When Tom shared his findings about the house with Tricia, she was even more excited to move into their new home on Madison Street and to experience the atmosphere of the past residents. She was as eager as Tom to dig deeper into the era of those first settlers that made Helena such a great place to live. She and Tom agreed that they would take next Tuesday to continue researching the background and history further.

PASTOR AARON AND JOHANNA GROSS

Meanwhile Opal was trying to adjust to the idea of moving from her home and establishing a new life so different from her past. In her memories she recalled the time when they purchased the house from Aaron and Johanna Gross. In 1890, after emigrating from Germany a few years earlier, the Gross family moved with their five children from New York to Helena. Their family was comprised of the oldest son Earnest, a second son Albert, and three girls, Jennifer, Rosemary and Heidi. Mr. Gross was eager to either help in establishing a church, or becoming a pastor. Later he did become the pastor of the First German Evangelical Lutheran Church. Their five children quickly filled the many rooms of the house with laughter, games and a bit of mischief.

After the children grew up and married, two of them moved to Bozeman and two moved to Billings. These towns were also growing with the wealth that gold brought.

After the death of his parents Earnest returned with his wife, Carol and their two children, Annette and Scottie, to live in the Painted Lady. Once again the laughter of children and their childhood adventures echoed within her walls. They experienced fun times and sad times while living amongst the memories of those who had lived there earlier. Earnest stayed in the home until he died and his wife went to live with their daughter. Another generation had left their memory footprint within the grand Painted Lady.

When Opal and her husband, Mike, purchased the house it needed some minor repairs, which Mike quickly mended. They were full of excitement and hopes for themselves and for a large family. Opal then remembered Tricia's enthusiasm for moving into the home with her dreams to fill the house with fun and happy times--- just like she and Mike had experienced. She stopped her reminiscing as her eyes began to mist and tears began to form. "Enough of this," she uttered, "I need to move on and leave this house behind."

Tricia was keen to learn more about the Gross family. She concentrated her research on this family. She discovered Johanna had Bible Story groups of young children in her home. The children sang little songs like *JESUS LOVES ME and MY LITTLE LIGHT*, and played games in the spacious back yard. The cookies that Johanna baked were so plentiful that most of the children preferred to stay until they were all consumed.

Johanna became acquainted, through their church, with the Erickson family who had recently moved from Iowa to homestead a large parcel of land some distance south of Helena. They had six children, the oldest of which was a girl of sixteen-named Dolly. She did attend school some but was unable to make the journey to and from home unless her dad took the wagon into town for supplies. The parents struggled financially to feed and clothe the children. Most of the money they had was put into raising enough wheat and other crops to meet the homestead requirements.

Johanna learned of the plight of the family and wanted to help in some way. She came up with a plan to ask Dolly if she would consider coming to work for her. Her duties would include helping with the laundry and other housekeeping. She discussed this idea with Dolly's mother beforehand assuring her that she had more housework than she could manage and truly needed help.

The Ericksons had two boys, Norman the oldest son, and Henry, the youngest of the boys. These two worked on other farms doing odd jobs to help provide income for the family. Dolly was consulted after her mother and Johanna had agreed that Dolly could be hired. Johanna also asked if she would like to spend the nights during the week with them since horseback was Dolly's only form of transportation. Johanna could bring her home on weekends. They agreed that Dolly would be paid five dollars a week and would have her meals with the Gross family. Mrs. Erickson thought the plans seemed a blessing and an answer to her prayer for additional income.

And so it was that Dolly came to be a part of the Gross family. She arrived the middle of May and immediately proved that she was a hard and conscientious worker. She even did chores that Johanna had not specified. The kids loved her because she found time to play with them. Many summer afternoons were spent in the backyard playing games like *Steal the Bacon* or *Hide and Seek*. Some Sunday afternoons included homemade ice cream and cookies. Sometimes Dolly joined them for this treat and then stayed overnight. The summer days were filled with laughter and fun; it seemed that the Gross family now had six beautiful children!

Johanna asked Dolly one day if she knew how to sew. "No, Mrs. Gross, Mom never has time to teach me very much. There are always so many chores for her to do that time for just one child is not possible. Besides I was needed to care for the younger ones."

"Well, how would you like for me to teach you? We could go to the mercantile and pick out some fabrics that you like and make you some dresses. What do you think?"

"That would be so wonderful, but I don't think I could use any money I make because my family really needs every little bit to help get by."

"That won't be a problem, Dolly, I will buy the fabric and you can make the dresses. Shall we do that soon so you can select the fabric you want and you can use your free time sewing?"

Dolly hardly knew what to say, and she eagerly agreed that learning to sew would be a wonderful thing to know. "Oh yes, Mrs. Gross, it will be so exciting to learn, and maybe I could learn to sew something for Mom." Dolly's eyes were tearing as Johanna reached out to give her a big hug.

A trip to the mercantile was soon arranged and Dolly eagerly awaited the day that she would see the selection of all the beautiful fabrics. She could choose the ones she liked best. After selecting a pink and green rose pattern and a bright blue one with yellow daisies, the two of them selected a pattern that would be just perfect for the material. The purchases were quickly wrapped. Dolly was eager to hurry back and get started on this new opportunity.

The following day Dolly quickly finished her chores. After measuring Dolly's size to the selected pattern, Johanna laid the pattern on the fabric, matching the design of the flowers. Then Dolly took the scissors and carefully cut around the pattern pieces. The pieces were then ready to be sewn together. Johanna sat down at the treadle sewing machine with Dolly seated beside her. Johanna took one piece and matching it to the appropriate section where it was to be joined, she began sewing. Dolly watched intently as Johanna sewed two more pieces together and then Johanna said, "Your turn now, Dolly." Under Johanna's close supervision Dolly began to sew two pieces at the proper seam lines. When she finished her eyes grew wide with excitement to think that she was learning how to sew. They took a break to prepare dinner. Dolly carefully laid the pieces she had sewn tenderly in the drawer, as if she was tucking a baby under blankets. This was something that she had done with her own hands. A whole new world was opening up before her!

Pastor Gross' church was scheduled to have their annual potluck picnic at a local park. Everyone was excited. The young people and children were especially eager because there would be lots of fried chicken, potato salad, roasted corn, watermelon, and bountiful produce from the family gardens. Rounding out the menu was all kinds of homemade bread and lots of pies and cakes. Johanna always brought her apple strudel and mincemeat pies because that was a favorite of all who came. It was the recipe that her grandmother and mother always made. Johanna could mix it together with her eyes closed because she had made it so many times. The aroma and flavor never failed to bring out the tantalizing spices that filled the many layers of finely sliced apples baked to perfection in a luscious smooth filling.

Johanna invited Dolly to go to church with them on the picnic day and stay for the feast after services; it would give her an opportunity to meet some other young people. There was another plan in Johanna's mind. She wanted to introduce Dolly to Mrs. MacPherson, a schoolteacher at Bryant School on Boulder Street. She was sure Mrs. MacPherson would be willing to tutor Dolly on some afternoons or evenings at home so Dolly could catch up on the missed education. Living so far out of Helena would make tutoring too difficult to commute. She felt that Dolly was quick enough to learn and should be able to return to school in the fall at her grade level.

At the Potluck the following Sunday, Johanna spotted Mrs. MacPherson shortly after she arrived and was quick to make her way to where Mrs. MacPherson was placing her food on the table. Johanna quickly engaged her in friendly chatter and then broached the subject of tutoring Dolly.

"Jean, have you heard that we have a lovely young girl working for us? She is a wonderful help and is eager to learn new things. She is the Erickson's daughter. The Ericksons live on a ranch quite a distance from Helena. The family came to Montana from Iowa and they are struggling to make their ranch sustainable. Due to the distance from town, Dolly, who is sixteen, does not have transportation to town and is unable to attend school. She currently spends the week living with us, going home only on the weekends. She seems very bright and hungry to learn, I was wondering if you would be willing to tutor her for an hour or two some afternoons after school? Hopefully she could be ready to enter her appropriate grade in the fall."

Jean responded, "Yes, I have heard of Dolly and her family and their struggles to maintain their ranch. It is my understanding that they have a large family. I would consider tutoring her if my classroom work is not too demanding, maybe two afternoons a week might work. I would need to evaluate her on her previous schooling in order to determine what materials are needed. Discuss with Dolly subjects she would like to learn and we'll see what we can work out. Certainly, I will do what I can."

While Johanna and Mrs. MacPherson were making plans for Dolly, Jennifer and Dolly were visiting with other young people from the church, and one in particular was a teenage lad named Jack. Immediately he started a conversation with Dolly and the two of them became engrossed in animated discussion. Jennifer was keeping her eye on another young man named Michael and the four of them agreed to be partners in a sack race. Johanna observed that her two charges were at the age when boys were beginning to take center stage in their attention.

JENNIFER'S FAIRY STORY

The changes in Jennifer's body surprised her. Her attitudes and moods shifted from tomboy days to focusing on boys. She made changes in her appearance directing her attention to becoming more attractive.

These changes were happening on a daily basis. Jennifer first noticed the bodice on her dresses becoming too tight. Her waist was retreating firmly into her body, and her feet were too big. Why should she care? She had always played baseball with her bothers, dug earthworms for fishing, and climbed tall trees with the best of the boys. Strange things were happening to her. Boys were a treat rather than a threat. Michael became center stage in her mind now. He was tall, though a bit gangly, and certainly good looking. She liked the way he smiled at her and he always arrived at church early to find a seat next to her. Sometimes, though, he did say silly things, especially when the two of them were alone. Her reaction to him was a fluttering heartbeat, like nothing she had ever experienced before. Sometimes she preferred the way things used to be; hiking with Ernest or swimming in the river with both brothers. But now she preferred Michael's company without others around.

Jennifer took these new changes with little notice, until one sunny summer afternoon Michael stopped by with plans for a picnic suggesting a quiet spot by the river for just the two of them. Johanna was hesitant at first to let Jennifer to go with him. Michael assured her he would take good care of her, bringing her home promptly by 3:00. Johanna knew Michael's family and, knowing them to be honest moral people, trusted Michael's promise.

Jenifer chose a lavender sundress with purple violets embroidered around the neck and bodice. A purple satin ribbon fit snugly around her waist accenting her developing feminine features. She deliberately chose this dress knowing the effect it would have on Michael. She felt in control of how the day would unfold. It was a thrilling sense of being female. She sensed that she had stepped over the threshold of being a girl into the awesome prospect of becoming a desired and respected woman.

They found a big flat boulder that overhung the edge of the river. Other smaller boulders pushed the water into surging currents, creating a small eddy by the shore. This was a perfect place to observe the small fish and larger trout swimming peacefully. It also was a perfect spot to dip their toes in the pool.

They finished the meat pies Michael's mother had prepared for them. They had almost eaten all the peanut butter cookies when Jennifer asked Michael, "What do you want to do when you finish high school? Do you want to go to college or do you have other plans?"

Michael thought for a moment and then answered, "I want to learn how to build big and beautiful bridges, especially like the Brooklyn Bridge in New York City. Bridges are both strong and awesome in their design, and I want to learn how to design and build bridges like that. In a way, it would be like having my name etched on the bridges that I build. I realize that I will have to attend college and take engineering courses to learn how to accomplish my dream. What are your plans?"

Jennifer thought for a minute and replied, "I want to become an illustrator for children's books. Actually, I want to write stories for children to learn how to be kind to animals and people. For instance, I see fairies living in the woods, flitting among the flowers. They stop to sip nectar from each flower like a honeybee. They poke their heads into a flower, and emerge dusted with pollen, teasing and laughing to each other. With mischief in her eye, one fairy steals a bit of a garden spider's web to make a swing in the trees. The tooth fairy takes baby teeth hidden under pillows and uses them to make a pathway for tiny toads to find a rain puddle. I want to bring laughter into the dreams of children. The fairies will laugh and giggle among themselves as they tickle the noses and cheeks of the dreamers. Reading these stories will create happy thoughts in a child's mind, building an awareness of happiness and love for others."

Michael sat quietly for a few minutes before responding to her. He was awed at her perception of nature and how it can create joy for children. "Jen, do you sketch these novel ideas just occasionally, or is this something you do every day?"

Jennifer laughingly replied, "I draw all the time. I have a sketchbook I use when I sit by the window and look out to the woods. On one stormy day when the lightening streaked across the sky with thunder crashing, I imagined brave little men in the woods fighting dragons. Then lots of horses came stampeding across my mind. The atmosphere was charged with anger and fright. The stories in my mind on that day were of heroic battles being fought for good against evil. But mostly I like drawing animals and make-believe characters. I envision children listening to my stories with rapt attention and excitement. That makes me feel alive."

Michael was so caught up listening to her he envisioned how children would be held spellbound hearing her colorful stories. "That is awesome. I think you should start saving all your sketches and stories storing them in a box, to be published later."

They suddenly realized that it was getting late and Michael was keen to keep his promise to Jennifer's mother. He did not want to jeopardize his chances to be with Jennifer by being irresponsible. They quickly gathered their shoes, the picnic blanket and some left over cookie crumbs and headed toward the home.

After dinner that evening, Jennifer retired to her room and curled up on her bed. She realized that Michael's idea of storing her sketches and stories in a box would indeed enable her to later assemble them as a children's book.

The next day she found just the right size box and hurried to her room. She gathered all her stories and sketches and placed them in the box. This would keep them all together and safe. She placed the box on the top shelf of her closet, pushing it all the way into the back corner. But Jennifer would not live to see her dreams realized. Three years later, in a hurry to go downstairs, she twisted her ankle and fell head first down the entire flight of stairs. She broke her neck severing her spinal cord. She died instantly. It would be many years later when her stories would come alive and echo as whisperings in the walls.

* * * * *

Days later Johanna called Dolly to her side as she was fixing dinner and began to discuss the idea for Dolly to begin a catch-up on her education.

"What would you think about having a school teacher come here one or two afternoons a week to help you attain the education that you have missed when you were unable to attend school?"

Dolly stopped chopping the vegetables and a quizzical look came on her face. "How would that be possible since I am not sure what things I have missed in my absence from school?"

"Mrs. MacPherson, from our church, has agreed to meet with you and determine what you would need to learn in order to enter the school year next fall with Jennifer. You are a very bright girl and Mrs. MacPherson will quickly recognize your ability."

Dolly sat down to ponder this idea before she responded. "I think that would be okay, but I don't think I will be able to do my assigned chores and have the time needed to study. I certainly would not want to fall behind doing my chores. I am willing to try this and see how the time works out; maybe I can do both the work and studying or maybe it won't work out. I would like to try this to see how I can manage my time."

"Of course you can, and do not fret about doing all the chores on time, I am sure that we can make arrangements for you to work around studying time. Perhaps some of the chores can be done earlier in the morning or later in the evening."

"Do you think Jennifer would be willing to help me?" Dolly was still trying to digest this new idea of adding a new project to her existing responsibilities.

"Oh, I'm sure she would love to help you. The two of you have developed a lovely friendship. Why not ask her and see if the two of you can work out a schedule for studying and doing chores.

At this suggestion, Dolly's face brightened with enthusiasm and she was eager to launch into this next phase of her life with the Gross family.

After each girl finished their daily chores, Dolly and Jennifer got their lessons and sat down at the dinning room table. Studying like this was fun and not so tiresome as when doing it alone. Once they established the routine they sat down together every day at 4:00 and worked until finished. Jennifer was an immense help to Dolly as she struggled at times to understand a problem. It was a wonderful working arrangement making their friendship stronger. They had become best pals.

Christmas was coming and the Gross family home was busy as a beehive getting ready with decorating and baking. Albert, Earnest and their dad were on a mission to find and cut down just the right tree for the living room. It was voted that they should find one that reached the ceiling this year. Jennifer, Heidi and Rosemary sat down to string popcorn for garlands for the tree and colorful paper chains to hang over the fireplace. Last year's ornaments were hauled down from the attic. The excitement was palpable as the air was filled with the aroma of cookies baking. Johanna made traditional German Christmas cookies like Zimtsterne, Pfeffernusse, Lebucken, the ones with all the heavenly spices rolled into the dough. Perhaps the favorite of all was the Bethmannchen made with marzipan that just melted in your mouth.

Although Dolly could not be with the Gross family for Christmas she joined in the preparation and decorating, sharing in the excitement before she left to be with her family.

Presents were wrapped and hidden from peering eyes. The children looked for clues as to what to expect under the tree. Each of the children was making surprise items for each other and for their parents.

When the boys and their father brought back a tall dense tree, there were shouts of joy and excitement. This was a perfect large tree to decorate. All hands were on board as they began adding the ornaments, lights and homemade trappings. All afternoon they were as busy as beavers putting everything just where it should be. Mom brought a pot of hot chocolate and cinnamon sticks when they finally sat down to admire their work. The only thing left to do was hanging the stockings on the fireplace mantel. Now they had only four more days to wait until that magical Christmas morning!

Snow had fallen during the night and they awoke to a winter wonderland. No one was interested in eating breakfast, they only wanted to bundle up and plunge into the deep snow. The snow was perfect for making snow angels, or for building a fort, and certainly to use their one sled. After the forts were quickly formed, snowballs began flying through the air. Laughter and screams from being hit with snowballs echoed throughout the entire backyard. They stopped for only thirty minutes to eat a hot dog and then rushed back outside,

When darkness began to fall, they finally gave up and trooped into the kitchen, wet, with rosy cheeks, soggy mittens and boots brimmed with crusted snow. They were not allowed to come inside and sit down until they had taken off their coats, caps and boots and placed them on the racks in the enclosed back porch. After removing their wraps they were greeted with large mugs of steaming spiced tea and thick slices of warm bread smeared with apple butter. This would be a day to be remembered forever by everybody.

During the night another six inches of snow fell and when the household awoke a breathtaking world of dazzling white greeted them. The children grabbed their heavy outdoor clothes and started for the door. But Mother stopped them in their tracks declaring they would have to eat a hot bowl of oatmeal first. She had sprinkled the oatmeal with brown sugar and a dollop of thick cream. They reluctantly sat down at the table and, at first toyed with the hot cereal, eager to go outdoors. After a couple of bites, however, they realized how hungry they were and soon devoured their share and asked for more.

Once outside the children were adrift in the deep snow plowing through the drifts to make a path, throwing snowballs, and just reveling in the joy of being buried in a vast blanket of white fluff. They decided to make a right jolly snowman and immediately the boys began to form a big ball, then a smaller one and finally the smallest one for the head. Admiring their handiwork they scrounged for things to make a face. Jennifer suggested that they could get dried crab apples from the tree in the backyard for eyes. Small twigs were gathered from bushes to make eyebrows. Ernest donated four of his red marbles for a lipstick mouth but nobody could come up with an idea for a nose. In desperation they went to Mother for some helpful ideas. She suggested that they could check in the basement for some gourds that had been gathered last summer. Perhaps they could break off the long end of a gourd and use that. After thoroughly sorting through the gourds in the basement they agreed on one with a stem that had a twisted crook. This would give the snowman, which was turning into a snow lady, a distinctive look like no other in the neighborhood.

Finishing the face, Rosemary suggested that one of Mother's old bonnets they had used for dress-up could be the final touch. And she knew just where a *stash* of old clothes was stored in the attic. To retrieve the bonnet she would have to take off her snow boots and heavy coat before Mother would allow her to go to the attic to get the bonnet. She suggested that they finish the rest of this goofy snowman later when she could return with the prized hat. They all stood back to admire their handiwork and agreed it was great so far, but they needed to find the right sticks for the arms. Scrounging around in the bushes they found two limbs that had curly twigs at the end. This would give the appearance of fingers reaching out to shake hands. Heidi suggested using red paint for the fingertips of the twigs. She remembered paint was left after Father painted the birdhouse. She thought the red tips would make the snow creature glamorous. It would be her responsibility to get the paint and polish each tip of the twigs. When all the pieces were in place, they stood back to admire this creation. Heidi suggested this should be snow girl instead of the everyday snow MAN. This was a novel idea and it was agreed to christen this master piece a snow GIRL If this was a girl then she needed a purse. Once again Rosemary said that she would make it her mission to get mother's big old purse. Jennifer offered one more suggestion "Let's get some tomato sauce and put a tablespoon on both cheeks making her a real knock out!"

They trooped in for a lunch of hot chicken noodle soup and thick slices of homemade bread. Mother allowed each one two cookies after lunch. Before tackling her list of chores Rosemary stole up to the attic and selected a bonnet and a big old black purse. She noticed a pair of black gloves that had been stored away in the box. She picked them up, thinking this would complete the outfit. Tucking them beneath her coat, she slipped into her room to hide her treasures and then hurried downstairs to do her chores.

Just before sunset Rosemary sneaked out to put the bonnet on the snow girl. She also had chosen a skinny red belt to hang the black purse on. She loosely snugged the belt with the attached purse around the lady's icy waist. She couldn't decide where to put the gloves so she placed them dangling halfway out of the purse. Jennifer had completed her mission supplying the tablespoons of tomato sauce. The goofy snow girl was now ready for the bright morning sun to spotlight their magnificent lady creation.

After finishing up in the kitchen Johanna donned her snow boots and a woolen jacket to go outside to get the mail. When she saw the snow creature she laughed as she studied what the children had fashioned. She decided that if this *thing* was to be a girl then she needed more feminine touches. After collecting the mail, she went into the kitchen and took one of her bib aprons, plucked a mop head from the closet, and, without taking off her coat and boots, returned to the snow creature. Carefully she put the bib over the bonneted head and drew the apron over the fat tummy tying the sash behind. She also took the gloves loosely hanging from the purse and put them into the apron pocket. When the dirty mop head was placed under the bonnet on the snow lady, Johanna stood back to admire her contribution. Convinced that the work was perfect she declared, "Now you are a proper woman for this neighborhood."

After dinner each of the children took turns taking a warm bath and after being toweled down they grabbed their nightclothes and went straight to bed. No one argued to stay up late!

CHRISTMAS WITH THE GROSS FAMIY

When the household was quiet Johanna and Aaron sat down to plan how to introduce their gift to the children on Christmas morning. Aaron had overheard a conversation with the men at the church. Abe Jenkins was talking about his female Bernese dog's puppies. She had eight puppies and he was wondering where he could find homes for all of them. When Aaron came home that evening sharing this news with Johanna they discussed the possibility of getting one of the puppies for Christmas morning. The dogs were born the first week of November and they would be old enough to adopt by Christmas. After discussing this possibility, they decided a puppy would be the perfect surprise for Santa's gift for the children.

Once the decision was made Aaron and Johanna selected a furry little male puppy. Arrangements were made for Mr. Jenkins to bring the puppy to the their house Christmas morning. He agreed to put the little dog in a box with a ribbon on the top and deliver it. This puppy was a loveable teddy bear of a dog that would be a perfect playmate for the children. When he grew to be the big dog he was bred to be, he would be fun to wrestle with and play games with the children. They were as excited as the children would be.

The next two days were busy in the kitchen making cookies, stollen, cinnamon rolls, gingerbread men and their favorite Christmas jam cake. The house was enveloped in the heady fragrance of sweet things, as preparations for holiday fun, family love, and all-you-can-eat goodies began. On Christmas Eve Johanna made taffy, giving everyone a turn at pulling big pieces of taffy then cutting them into bite-sized pieces. 'Course the children sneaked a piece or two when no one was looking.

Knowing that Santa would come only if everyone was asleep in bed, the younger children eagerly donned pajamas and climbed between piles of comforters and quilts. After saying prayers and climbing into bed, mom and dad kissed each one reminding them how much they were loved. Albert, Earnest and Jennifer were allowed to stay up a bit longer before saying good night and headed off to their dreams.

Aaron and Johanna pulled their chairs up to the warm fireplace, cradling a cup of tea, and basking in the love that filled their home. God had provided for all their needs. Their thoughts drifted toward Dolly's family and their preparation for the holidays. The Ericksons had raised a small herd of cattle to sell. Dolly told them that the family was doing better financially. They had produced a bountiful garden and Dolly's mother had canned enough vegetables and along with their beef they had ample provisions for the winter.

"We should take a large basket of pastries and jellies and jams to them tomorrow," said Johanna as she squeezed Aaron's hand.

"Most certainly," Aaron agreed "and let's take the children with us. I know that Jennifer has made a special gift for Dolly and will want to give it to her personally." They prayed together, extinguished the coals, sighed heavily, and they too went to bed.

Christmas morning dawned bright and cold. The children, en mass, came running down the stairs almost knocking over the tree as they jockeyed for a place by the tree. Father designated, one at a time, who would take a present from under the tree and give it to the person whose name was on the package. It seemed so agonizingly slow but finally everybody had opened his or her gifts. Earnest had received two cars for his train set; Albert was thrilled with his backpack and hunting knife and was eager to take off to the woods. Jennifer got a beautiful new dress with lace on the sleeves and around the waist. Heidi got a big doll with long auburn curls with a complete outfit for her. Rosemary could hardly believe her eyes when she saw the beautiful wooden cradle her father had made for her dollie. Mother had made three outfits and two colorful blankets for her baby doll and placed them into the new cradle. The excitement was at a high pitch with everyone chattering at once about the wonderful gifts they had received.

As the din subsided there was a knock at the front door. No one was interested in being interrupted from his or her fun to answer the door, so Father got up to open the door. He stepped outside quickly closing the door behind him. Carefully taking the prized box, he thanked Mr. Jenkins for delivering this special package. Nobody noticed the package he brought in until he carefully set the wiggling box on the floor.

"Look, we have a package from Santa," Father shouted loudly to the noisy group seated on the floor.

All eyes turned to see what Father had brought. When he tilted the box on its side the furry contents came tumbling out on the floor. First there was an awed silence, and then squeals of joy pierced the air. Everyone dropped their gifts and scrambled to gather the puppy up in their arms. The room was wild with the happy cries of all the children, young and old.

Father quickly brought the chaos under control designating a time for each child to hold the puppy. The little guy was overwhelmed with the noise and the pressing bodies around him. The joy of having this little one seemed to flood the room as each rushed to scoop him up in their arms. Wet kisses and puppy slobber spilled over onto their faces as they nuzzled against his furry body. Never would there be a greater gift than this. All other gifts were cast aside as they each took turns playing with this furry puppy. In the midst of this hubbub everyone sensed the presence of Jesus, aware of the many blessings that He had showered upon them. They were especially thankful for the gift of this wiggly armful of fur.

All eyes were fixed on the puppy as they began seeking names for the little one. Names like Browser, Titan, Tommy, Hercules, Happy, Tiger, came tumbling out of their mouths. So many names were suggested, with everyone talking at once. That is until Rosemary said, "Hansel as in the fairy story of Hansel and Gretel." In the silence the children began to mouth the name HANSEL Their approval rose in unison. So it was that this handsome black dog with a brown mask around his eyes and nose and a white patch on his chest was to be HANSEL, the newest member of their family. What wonderful gift from God!

Winter enjoyed a long stay in Helena, but the month of May began nudging the cold aside to bring forth early flowers, announcing that summer was not too far behind. The Gross family seemed to take on a new breath of life as they ventured outdoors. Their days quickly were filled with activities, and making plans for the summer. Hansel, no longer the cuddly puppy, had grown by leaps and bounds! He was now an awkward teenager growing fast to fill his huge paws. When the weather permitted, all the children and Hansel were constantly outside playing.

On a warm May morning, Heidi was in school waiting for the recess bell that would allow her and her friend to play outside. When the bell rang, the fourth and the fifth grade class were dismissed for a thirty-minute break. Heidi and her friend Katherine were one of the first to claim their favorite spot on the playground. After catching their breath they excitedly shared their plans for the summer. Katherine said, "my folks are taking me to the Yellowstone Park. Everyone is talking about the wonders of the place with the spouting geysers and hot water pools. There are all kinds of wildlife there. It is all my parents talk about since it became a national park. I am so excited to see all this! What are your plans Heidi?"

Heidi was in the process of telling her about visiting Dolly at the ranch to go horseback riding. "You remember Dolly, don't you? She was the girl who stayed with us to help Mother. She has returned to her family and has asked me to visit." Heidi was telling Katherine about the horses at Dolly's ranch when Ricardo, a big fifth grader stepped into their space and began teasing Heidi.

"You are that preacher's kid, aren't you? I bet you never have any fun at all. Your father probably keeps you at home to keep you out of trouble. You are Miss Goody Two Shoes and a spoiled brat".

Heidi immediately shouted back in his face "I do too have fun! My brothers and sisters take me places with them and we have fun doing things together all the time. Go away. Leave me alone." Smirking, Ricardo turned to leave, mocking her as he did so.

When Heidi came home after school, she had tearstains on her face and Jennifer immediately wanted to know what happened. Heidi sobbed out the events during recess and Jennifer gave her a big warm hug as only a big sister can. Albert and Earnest were in the kitchen eating apples and overheard this conversation. Albert took Earnest aside and said "We can do the one-two move on Ricardo to teach him a lesson not to pick on our little sister." Earnest nodded in agreement and they laid plans for the next school day.

The next day after school was over, the two brothers took their positions just outside the schoolyard and waited for Ricardo. It wasn't long before Ricardo came out with a couple of his buddies laughing and making fun of the girls. Albert called to Ricardo telling him they had something for him, inviting him to come and collect what they had for him. Earnest positioned himself to one side and behind as the bully came to where Alfred was waiting for him.

"What do you have that I could want from you?" Ricardo snarled when he came to face Albert.

"Oh, just a little souvenir from our sister Heidi." By this time Earnest had dropped to a bent position behind Ricardo. With one powerful swoop Albert shoved Ricardo backward causing him to fall on his back. Like lightening Earnest sprang on top of him pinning him to the ground slamming Ricardo's arms over his head. The one-two worked like a dream. Ricardo, stunned, started blubbering threats, but Earnest quickly stopped his words when he dropped heavily onto his chest, making it difficult for him to talk and breathe.

"Did I hear you offer an apology?" When no words came from Ricardo, Albert repeated the question, "I can't hear you telling us that you are sorry. Try again, only speak a bit louder."

This time Ricardo blurted out the words Albert was waiting to hear. "Okay, next time you want to talk about preacher kids come to us and leave our sister alone. Do you understand?"

When Ricardo was released from the strong hold of the two boys he quickly stumbled up and ran away.

ROSEMARY AND THE BEAR

June brought sunny days with hot temperatures and cool nights for sleeping. On such a June day Johanna asked the children if they would like to go for a picnic by the river. The boys could play catch or they could explore doing whatever they pleased. Of course it was unanimous, they wanted the freedom of being out in the wide-open spaces and with plenty of food to enjoy. Albert was especially keen to put his backpacking equipment to the test, especially his compass using his tracking skills. The girls were eager to search for wild flowers and if the clover in the fields had bloomed, they wanted to make a flower chain. The following Saturday Johanna packed a hearty lunch of sandwiches, cheese, fruit and cookies accompanied by a gallon of fruit punch.

Since the family owned only a carriage for transportation, Father borrowed a small wagon from Mr. Hanks, a church member, to take their family on a picnic by the river. Mr. Hank's wagon would accommodate all five children and picnic supplies necessary for a day's adventure. When all the family was seated in the wagon there was no room for Hansel. He didn't recognize that as a problem, and with one great leap he landed on top of all the children, settling in the *nest* of soft warm bodies. No one complained even though they were squeezed together like sardines in a can.

They had hardly gotten out of town when the girls began singing songs they had learned at school. Albert and Earnest didn't join because, in their opinion, that was not very manly! They chose instead to keep their eyes open for wild game; buffalo and deer were often seen roaming the plains. When they turned to go on a less traveled road to the meadows, Albert saw a covey of quail flush at the sound of their horse and wagon. Hansel also noticed and tried to scramble to the edge of the wagon, barking furiously. Everybody was in a tumble until they could quite him down. The tone of the day was laughter!

They picked a spot in an open field close to the river. There was a big pine tree close by and Johanna selected this as the perfect spot for the picnic. As soon as the horses stopped at the picnic spot children and dog poured out like molasses from a jar. It was a race to the river and Albert and Earnest, with their long legs, were the first to arrive at the river's edge. Then it was game on to see who could skip rocks the furthest across the river. Hansel wasted no time jumping in and the boys tossed him sticks to retrieve. After many trips to retrieve the sticks Hansel swam to shore, shook off the water and lay down panting in the sun to warm.

The girls preferred to search for clover and wild flowers. Rosemary thought the prettiest flowers were a bit further out in the field. Eager to pick a big bouquet for her mother she continued to wander further and further away from her sisters. No one noticed that she was slowly disappearing from sight. When Jennifer and Heidi had found enough clover blossoms to make chains, they challenged each other to see who could make the longest chain. They were totally preoccupied with their project and didn't realize Rosemary was nowhere in sight. They called to her but she did not answer. Panicking they quickly got up to search for her. Even though they continued further afield they couldn't find her. Jennifer was becoming concerned and said, "I think we should get Father and the boys to help look for Rosemary." Heidi was quick to agree and together they ran back to the family seated under the pine tree.

As soon as the girls arrived, Hansel sensed that Rosemary was missing. He was the first to greet Heidi and Jennifer. When the girls related their concerns about Rosemary, Father and the boys were up and on their way with Hansel leading the way. He bounded ahead picking up Rosemary's scent. Since the others couldn't keep up with him, Hansel would turn frequently to see if they were still following him and take off running again. It seemed they had walked miles and still were unable to find Rosemary.

Rosemary, meanwhile, finally realized that she had wandered too far out of sight and could no longer see her sisters. She tried retracing her steps, but with the grass so high she was not able to see the path she had taken. She realized that she was lost. Her wandering path had led her into the surrounding woods and she could no longer see the meadow. Her first thought was to sit down and wait for someone to find her. She had been sitting for some time when she heard a rustling in the bushes behind her. At first, she could not see anything and thought it must be the leaves rustling in the breeze. She turned to look for the noise but saw nothing. When the noise stopped she was sure that her imagination was playing tricks on her, so she relaxed.

Hansel was long out of sight and Father was frustrated thinking that Hansel was no longer following her scent. Father wondered if he was off chasing rabbits or birds. The troop continued searching for signs of where Rosemary could have stopped or walked off in another direction. They kept calling her name every few feet but got no answer. Father was becoming increasingly worried and picked up his pace almost to a run. Both boys were right behind him scanning the area hoping to find Rosemary.

It wasn't long before Rosemary spotted the cause of the noise. A large brown bear had ambled into the area where she was, and he was about ten feet from her. He was searching for berries as he slowly ambled toward her. Rosemary froze praying as hard as she could for God's protection. The bear grunted and stopped to determine what was directly in front of him. When the bear stood up on his hind legs to look at her, Rosemary realized how tall he was—much taller than Father. He growled and hesitated, not sure what to do in this situation. As he came closer to see what was in front of him, Rosemary saw his huge size and his big teeth. She closed her eyes waiting for the bear to crunch her with his powerful jaws. But the bear did not come any further because Hansel was there at her side barking with fury and anger. The bear stopped in his tracks not coming any closer to Rosemary. But that wasn't good enough for Hansel. Growling and barring his teeth he ran toward the bear, snapping at his heels always staying out of reach of those powerful paws. The bear made a bluff charge but stopped when Hansel did not retreat, growling as he pawed the air. Again, Hansel was on the offensive lunging and barking fiercely. The bear turned and made a run for the woods with Hansel close behind.

When the bear had disappeared into the woods, Hansel returned to Rosemary, covering her with wet kisses. Rosemary threw her arms around Hansel's neck loving him and thanking him for saving her life. Hansel began pacing back and forth, telling her to follow him back to the family. She wasted no time in scrambling to her feet and staying close beside Hansel as he led her out of the woods and into the meadow. They had gone only a short distance when Rosemary saw Father and her brothers making their way toward her. They ran to meet each other with tears and prayers of thanksgiving as they fell into each other's arms. Hansel was wagging all over and jumping around with joy. Father hugged his big furry neck and unashamedly kissed him.

When Rosemary shared her story about the bear, they all fell on Hansel's neck hugging and kissing him. It was then that Aaron and Johanna realized that their decision to get a puppy for their children was God's direction leading them. Hansel was indeed a gift from God.

CHANGING OF THE
GUARD FOR THE
PAINTED LADY

fter his parents had passed and the rest of the family had left home, Earnest, the oldest of the Gross boys, moved into the home place with his wife Carol and their two children, Annette and Scottie. Until then the old home sat empty looking like a forlorn old woman. If you listened closely you could hear her sighs of loneliness, holding her breath waiting for life to begin again.

Upon moving into this big house, the children were ecstatic; racing into each room with unbounded joy loving all the space to play. Their greatest joy was the discovery of the attic. Dolls, doll furniture, train set, balls, toy trucks and cars, and lots, lots and lots of room. The joyous sound of children within the walls of the old home renewed her life. She warmly welcomed this new family into her care. New lives would create memories within her walls.

However, a tragedy would unfold within the home when their young son, Scottie, died of scarlet fever complications.

Tricia would accidently discover this tragedy in the Earnest's family while cleaning the playroom attic many years later. Sorting and cleaning out the closet, she uncovered a box of toy soldiers with the poem Little Boy Blue by Eugene Fields tucked inside. She would later experience the sadness of one who had lived within these walls.

As Tricia further researched the Gross family, she discovered they were the most popular folks in the neighborhood. On summer afternoons the ladies in the neighborhood gathered for tea, and most often it was at Johanna's house. Her delicious sponge cake she served was a favorite.

Tom, meanwhile, was searching for the description of the exterior of the house. He wanted the house to be restored to its original beauty. Some of the spindles that held the railing to the wrap-around porch were missing. All that was left of the third story balcony were two posts without the railing. The stained-glass window on the third floor had a covering built over it so that would necessitate finding a company who could create an exact replicate of the original window. Tricia was the artist and she would doggedly pursue finding just the right company that could restore it perfectly. Tom also found that new gutters would need to be installed on all floors. The front porch flooring was in need of repair with a fresh coat of waterproofing. He found himself caught up in the excitement of moving in and getting to work returning this beautiful Painted Lady to her glorious past.

On the way home from the library Tom and Tricia stopped to pick up a couple of Arby's sandwiches. When they got home and seated themselves at the kitchen table, they hungrily devoured the sandwiches. Tricia paused as she picked up her iced tea and said, "Tom, I have been thinking about Opal and her sadness over leaving her home. I could tell that her heart was breaking having to leave.

I wonder if we could make some arrangement for her to have one of the big rooms on the main floor as her own. We could make the space into a small apartment with a private bath. The room is so large that these changes could be made easily without compromising the structure. She could use the porch side entrance. Just think, we could have the pleasure of hearing her past history and that of her family."

Tom put down his tea and reaching for a cookie, paused and said, "I think that might just work out. I, too, sensed that this is a traumatic crisis for her moving and adjusting to a different life with her daughter. I will speak with the contractor tomorrow about a plan for the apartment when we discuss his design for the expansion of the master bedroom and the spa bath. Why don't you check with Opal about this idea? I will inquire about an additional loan to incorporate these changes."

Having finished their small meal, they settled down on the overstuffed sofa and watched TV for a while. Tricia was so excited about this idea and eager to hear Opal's reaction. The excitement was too intense for her to go to sleep right away, so she remained in her chair mulling over their discussion. Tom stayed up crunching some figures to see how this new idea could be done. He would need to talk with the loan officer at their bank and see what finances could be arranged.

Tricia was up early after a fitful night's sleep, eager to contact Opal. She rang Opal asking if she could come to her house in about an hour. "I have some very exciting news to tell you," she said. Opal had just finished her toast and coffee and was taken a little aback at Tricia's excited tone of voice. "Yes, Dear. I suppose so. But not before 10:00 I need to change clothes and finish the breakfast dishes."

When the doorbell rang, Opal had not quite finished the breakfast dishes. Picking up a towel she dried her hands and answered the door. There stood Tricia with a smile as big as the morning sunrise. Opal had barely opened the door when Tricia burst into the room. She quickly sat down in one of the big overstuffed chairs, her hands moving excitedly as she blurted out her ideas.

"Oh Opal, I have something exciting to tell you! I hope you will be as excited as Tom and I are. We both felt the wave of nostalgia when you agreed to sell your home. It is understandable that it was a tearful decision. We have been discussing the purchase of the house and the changes we would like to make and it is our desire to make private quarters for you on the main floor. We want you to stay a part of this remarkable home since you are a vital part of its history. The walls contain warm memories of you and your family when you lived here. You are an integral part of this house reflecting its beauty with your own beauty. So, would you agree to either living here with us, or coming for long visits? This house would have its completeness with your presence."

Opal hardly had time to catch her breath upon hearing this proposal. Her answer was slow and somewhat stumbling, "My dear, this is a drastic change that you are offering. I am due to go to California with my daughter and to live with her. She has made arrangements to have an apartment made for me in her home. I think she would be disappointed if I changed her plans. Actually, any changes would have to be discussed with her. I do like the idea of having a room when I visit. I think it would be like coming home. However, an extended visit is not the best idea because it is easy to wear out your welcome if the visit is too prolonged."

Tricia didn't miss a beat with her response. "We anticipated how wonderful it would be to include you as part of our family. Only you could bring to life the warmth and passion residing in this home. You would be welcome to visit as long as you wish. We do understand your desire to live close to your daughter. By the way, we are looking forward to meeting your daughter and discussing plans that would be in your best interest."

"When Brenda arrives we can get together and discuss this

further. She will be pleased to know that you desire to have me visit and being with your family."

They both agreed they would get together when Brenda arrived. As she got up to leave, Tricia gave Opal a warm hug and was pleased that she received one in return.

Tricia went home with her mind whirling with eagerness to learn all she could about the painted lady. Now she could combine the earliest history of the Gross and Humphreys families with the history that Opal provided. This information would become a complete sketch of all the lives that had breathed, worked, and loved here. She felt she was being transported back in time as she experienced the emotions of this wonderful house. She wondered about the intense love the Gross and Humphreys couples had for each other and how it affected all who lived there. It was magical to imagine what it was like tucking each of the small children into bed each night, kissing their tiny cheeks and hearing those cooing words of love as they responded with giggles and big hugs. These precious times would quickly flee as the children grew up seeking their adventures of fun with some mishaps, and finally entering adulthood. There were mixed moments of joy and sadness swirled in a hearty mixture of emotions as each one left to find a life of their own. After each one married and left, family voices were no longer heard echoing within the walls. There would be no more laughter, just silence and emptiness and sadness hovering in the air. The parents felt pride, however, knowing they had done their best as each child ventured forth to find their place in life. Tricia wondered what the life of Opal's family would bring to this mixture of history.

Opal immediately called Brenda to explain the offer the Johnsons had made regarding fixing a special room in the house for her, saying, "I told them that we would have to discuss this to determine if this would be a workable situation. Tricia originally wanted to fix an apartment on the first floor of the house for me to move into, suggesting that I live with them. I didn't think this was the best thing to do. Instead, I suggested a room might be available for me when I visit, but not for prolonged periods of time. This is something that we need to sit down and work out together when you come. What are your thoughts?"

"Mom, I think you made a wise choice for two reasons. The first reason is I want you to spend more time with Chris and me. I have looked forward to this time when we can do things together. We can have time recalling the happy memories we have shared. We can have long chats, something that I have missed. The second reason, I think you might feel a bit out of place with others living in the house that once was yours and which you no longer own. Your suggestion for a visit is the best way to go."

"Chris and I are driving up in the SUV next Friday probably taking two or three days to get there. Start making mental notes of the things you want to bring to California. After choosing the things you want to bring back for the apartment we can ship any larger pieces or put them into storage until you decide what to do with them. This will relieve your stress and give you time to make decisions once you are settled in your apartment. Chris will drive the SUV with the U-Haul back to California taking your selected things and we can fly home whenever we are ready."

"That takes a worrisome responsibility off my mind, I just need someone to help me think things through and make wise decisions. I am just too old to be caught up in all this decision process. So, call me before you leave letting me know when you will arrive. I'll start putting some of my clothes and personal keepsakes in boxes. This will give us a head start on getting things ready to move. Honey, I love you so much for this and can hardly wait until you are here in person."

The following morning Brenda was finishing plans for the

apartment that she and Chris had set in motion if Opal came to live with them. All the major refurbishing was finished. The choice of colors, curtains and accessories would be Opal's decision. Brenda was so thrilled her mother was coming. This was a wish she had for many months, and now it was becoming a reality.

Dragging out two suitcases, Brenda sorted and began packing clothes for the two of them. She needed to make wise choices since she was unsure how long their stay would be. They would drive to Helena and Chris would rent a U-Haul to bring back the things Opal had chosen to put into the apartment. Brenda could stay as long as necessary with her mother and the two of them would fly back to California. Chris would assist in making arrangements for the things that needed to be stored. He realized Opal would have difficulty making decisions. It would be an emotional time for Opal to separate herself from her home and all the things that reminded her of the life she had with her family. He felt that storing most of her things for a while would give her some emotional space and time to decide about her future plans.

Rising early on Monday morning Brenda packed some granola bars, a few grapes, and some fig bars along with a thermos of hot coffee. One last thought caused her to put in some cheese and crackers in case they could not find a place for lunch. Chris came out of the shower, dressed and ready to start packing the car as Brenda was finishing the snacks. There was a bit of excitement as they were making final preparations. It had been a long time since the two of them had made the effort to get away alone to enjoy each other's company.

Before departing Brenda called Opal to say they were ready to leave and gave her the rough itinerary of their journey to Helena. She assured Opal she would call enroute and let her know where they were and how the trip was progressing. All the lights in the house were turned off, the shades were drawn, no leaky faucets, the paper cancelled and arrangements for their next-door neighbor to keep an eye on the place watching for any signs of trouble, had been taken care of. Their cell phones enabled them access to any urgent messages. Satisfied that everything was secured, they climbed into the car and with a sigh of relief, focused on the trip ahead.

There was something freeing about the bright sunlit morning and the fresh breezes filling the car that promised a good omen for their trip. They had planned a northern route along the Pacific coast and their destination for the first night was Ashland, Oregon. The next morning they hoped to have breakfast at a quaint little restaurant where they had once enjoyed delicious homemade cinnamon rolls as large as a plate. They had discovered this jewel on an earlier trip and they definitely intended to stop again for those huge yummy cinnamon rolls. Brenda remembered the large blooming pink rhododendron and fiery red azaleas covering the front of the building. Purple, pink and red petunias spilled out of flower boxes creating a riot of color. Brenda would have stopped there just to see the flowers, even if the cinnamon rolls weren't that great!

The following morning, they were well on their way to Portland and continued on to Clarkston, Idaho. It was their plan to drive over Lolo Pass where they planned to stop for the night at the hot springs located on the Montana side of the mountains. This was such beautiful country and Brenda suggested, "We should linger along the way just to drink in the beauty of the mountains in the Big Sky Country of Montana. Truly this is God's country so why not take a day to do some hiking??"

Chris was in total agreement. They stopped at the next trailhead, where they parked. Brenda dug through their packed things looking for an additional sweater or jacket for each of them so they could layer their clothes and keep warm if needed. The day was sunny and the heady fragrance of the pine and fir trees seemed to completely envelope them as they walked further into the woods. As they were walking they could see and hear the creek rushing over the rocks so they took a detour down to the edge of the creek. They found a large boulder and stopped for a break. Brenda pulled out the granola bars, and sighing said, "This kind of beauty could cause one to lose all the stress and concerns of life in this peaceful atmosphere." They watched, in a trance, as the creek rushed over the rocks spotting rainbow trout swimming in the swift current.

They lingered for quite some time, unaware of the clouds slowly drifting in over the mountains. When a cloud blotted out the sun they quickly noticed the difference in the temperature and realized it was time to return to the car. They drank deeply of the pungent fragrance of the forest tucking the memory of the gurgling creek into their minds for later recollection. Totally refreshed and relaxed they returned to the car and, removing their sweaters, settled in for the remainder of the trip.

After a quick lunch in Missoula they continued the uneventful journey to Helena. Taking turns driving, the miles seemed to disappear. Just as dark descended they entered the city limits. Since it was so late when they arrived they decided to spend the night in a motel and they would call Opal the next morning to tell her when to expect them.

Opal had a breakfast of sausage, hot biscuits and scrambled eggs waiting for them when they arrived. After a couple cups of steaming hot coffee, fortifying them with caffeine, they settled at the table and ate heartily. Opal nervously waited for them to finish breakfast so they could start discussing the tasks before them. Brenda noticed the lines of fatigue on Opal's face around her eyes. She seemed so weary. Brenda was concerned about her mother's health. Putting those observations in the back of her mind Brenda decided it best not to let Opal know that she was aware of the stressful signs that were written on her mother's face.

After everyone found a comfortable spot in the living room, they kicked off their shoes and stretched their cramped legs. Opal immediately began sharing all the events that had transpired. Brenda and Chris listened attentively as Opal described Tricia's proposal for having a room remodeled so she could stay in her home with the Johnsons. She explained that Tricia and Tom wanted to include her like a member of their family. Opal was wary of becoming that involved in a situation with people she did not know. She wanted Brenda to counsel her on the pros and cons of this type of arrangement.

"Mom, I guess I am selfish, but I don't want to share the rest of your life with anyone else but us. You are important to us and because we love you so much, I think it wise not to make a hasty decision. Maybe you could come for a visit when you feel like traveling." Opal sighed with relief, thankful she had someone to help her make this difficult decision. Opal planned to call Tricia and set a time when all of them could discuss this further. Opal would tell her the decision at that time. Once this was decided, Opal felt she could finally relax and stop worrying knowing that the situation was taken care of.

Chris brought their luggage into the house, picked up the fresh towels and sheets Opal had placed by the steps, and carried everything upstairs to their bedroom. After Opal's call, Tricia was eager to meet Brenda. They quickly established a meeting time for the next day at Opal's home. Tricia arrived promptly at 2:30 and was warmly greeted by Opal and Brenda. After introductions they settled in the living room. They chatted for a few minutes and then Opal offered cranberry scones and English Teatime tea. Brenda immediately felt a warm connection with Tricia and their conversation got off to a friendly start.

"I have been so eager to meet you," Tricia began. "Opal has shared so much about you I feel I have known you for a long time. I am sure Opal has shared our desire to have your mother stay with us. The house must feel like her family and we can understand her reluctance to leave this part of her life behind. Selfishly, we would love to have her living with us and hearing stories about her life in this house."

Brenda smiled and replied, "It is kind of you to want Mother with you and certainly she has a treasure trove of family history and memories. But, we too, want her to be a part our lives. Your offer for her to share the home with you is a generous one and shows the compassion that you have for her. We think at his time in Mother's life she should be with us. At a later time if she is able to fly, she could return for a visit and stay in the room prepared for her. We both are honored that you consider her an integral part of your family. Please understand our decision is for Mother's well being. We do not want you to think we are ungrateful. Your thoughtfulness has touched our hearts."

"Sure, I understand that she would want to be with her children," Tricia replied. "She is such a charming lady whose company we would enjoy and never grow tired of talking with her. She enhances the beauty of this great house with her own special beauty."

"Opal, may I have another one of those scrumptious scones? You are such an excellent cook. Brenda, you know from experience, there will be special goodies pouring out of your kitchen when Opal comes to live with you. I envy that." Tricia laughingly added.

The topic of conversation changed as Brenda shared a bit about her life in California. She elaborated on the plans for Opal's apartment. After they finished eating the scones and had refreshed their cups of tea a few times, Tricia asked Opal to stay in touch. Tricia was interested to know how she was adapting to her new life. She certainly wanted to maintain the friendship that had developed between them.

"Of course, I will contact you after I settle down at Brenda's. I want to know how you are treating my *painted lady* with your new ideas and upgrades." Opal replied.

Tricia got up to leave, and Opal reached out and gave her a hug and was warmly hugged in return. Tricia said she would call when the title and all other papers were ready for signature.

Opal walked Tricia to the door and watched as she walked down the path to her car. Soft fingers of past memories drifted cross her mind. Standing there she recalled the many times she watched her children skip down the same path on their way to school. Those were such warm memories, just like loving arms gently enfolding her. The realization that those bygone days had turned into reality gave her chills. Now the unknown future ahead brought her face-to-face with a new life without the security of her husband and family. It was as if death had pulled the foundation from under her and she was falling into oblivion grasping for something to hold onto. Clasping the door she steadied herself, willing herself to face what lay ahead. She reminded herself this was the way she always handled crisis when life had forced demands and change upon her.

Brenda came to her side and put her arms around her sensing she was having difficulty coming to terms with this new phase of her life. It was frightening to realize the only life she knew was disappearing into the past. Both of them had tears in their eyes. It seemed the only thing to do was to hold each other tightly and let their emotions spill out. They would do the necessary things tomorrow when their emotions had run its course.

Brenda suggested that they go to the Chinese restaurant in town that evening for dinner. "I remember they had the best sweet and sour chicken." Chris came downstairs to join them. Hearing the plan for Chinese food he quickly agreed to this excellent idea. "I'll be ready as soon as I take a quick shower and we can arrive before the crowd begins to fill the place," he said. "I'm starved and Chinese food sounds great."

Dinner WAS great and they felt so much better with full

tummies. The atmosphere was not so gloomy as the emotional stress faded "Let's stop and get some chocolate chip mint ice cream to take home," Brenda said. "Let's be reckless and get some hot fudge topping to pour over our ice cream. We'll blow away any calories attached to it. "Let's assume the future will turn out to be exactly what we want it to be." This was the perfect ending for the day with its trauma and they left for home cheered by this extravagance.

Tricia called the following morning to tell them that the papers would be ready in five days. She suggested that they meet at the title office to sign the papers.

Opal, Brenda and Chris rose early the next morning to begin the arduous task of sorting, deciding what things to take in the U-Haul and what things to place in storage. There was a consignment company available if they chose to sell some things. Opal asked Brenda to advise her what furniture would best fit into her apartment. It was obvious that her bed and dresser, a small nightstand, several lamps, a few pictures and her favorite rocker were necessary items. She wanted to take her favorite quilts, the ones she had made years ago for the family. Opal asked Brenda if her big stuffed chair would fit in the space, she would leave the big sofa. They both agreed to take a desk that had been in the family for generations. It seemed the decision-making process was endless. Opal finally called a time out. They all headed for the kitchen for coffee and after quickly making sandwiches, they propped up their weary feet up and breathed a sigh of relief.

It was sad to part with things connected with her life. The stress of those two days left Opal completely exhausted and emotionally drained. Chris started packing the U-Haul. It soon became evident that there wasn't enough room to take all the things that Opal had selected to go with her. They spent another afternoon selecting things to put into the van. Some things were placed in storage for a later decision on what to do with them. It was difficult to tell if they were making any progress getting Opal ready to move, but they preserved. After a week of these exhausting times of decisions, packing and collapsing in sheer fatigue, they decided that enough was enough and whatever had been selected and packed would go. The remainder would be placed in storage for later decisions or for the consignment agent.

The day to sign the papers for the sale of the house was overcast increasing Opal's foreboding of leaving her beautiful *painted lady*. Arriving at the title office that morning at 10:00 they all sat down to take care of business. Opal, with shaky hands and trembling voice, signed each page as directed. As soon as the transaction was completed, Tricia suggested that they come to their house to celebrate with a bottle of champagne and mini snacks. Opal begged off, she only wanted to return home to rest.

Brenda apologized for not accepting the offer and told Tricia, "This has been a difficult time for Mother and I think she will need time alone to adjust to leaving her home." Tricia replied, "I completely understand. Perhaps we can get together to say good-bye before you leave. We want to make sure that we have your address and telephone number making sure we won't lose contact with you. Please encourage Opal to come back to visit us when she is able to travel. All of you are most welcome to come and stay with us when we have finished renovating."

Not knowing when their paths would cross again Tricia exchanged hugs with Opal and Brenda.

Within a few days all the sorting and packing was finished and Chris was ready to leave for home. Brenda made plane reservations for her and Opal. They would leave five days later. Chris would pick them up at the airport. During the remaining time in the house, Opal was quiet and somewhat downcast. However, her attitude rebounded and she wore her usual smlle with a spirit of anticipation as they boarded their plane.

OPALS MEMORIES

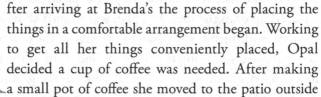

After arriving at Brenda's the process of placing the things in a comfortable arrangement began. Working to get all her things conveniently placed, Opal decided a cup of coffee was needed. After making a small pot of coffee she moved to the patio outside her apartment. The warmth of the sun lulled her body into a drowsy state of peace. To have sunshine for most days was a new treat. She took advantage of this sunny morning to relax while sipping her coffee. Thoughts of all that had transpired in the days and weeks since moving to Brenda's began to morph into new reality. It wasn't as difficult as she had imagined, in fact she was enjoying the change and the advantages of having her daughter near. She relished the renewed closeness that she developed with Brenda, something that had been missing when they lived so far apart.

MIKE'S ADVENTURES

Settling into her cozy big chair she retrieved the family photo album and slowly turned the pages. Staring at her on the first page was a goofy picture of Mike. He had been on the roof shoveling snow. There had been a heavy snowstorm the night before and Mike was concerned that the roof might not be able to withstand the weight of the additional snow. Fully clothed in a big coat, a wool hat covering his ears, and thick woolen gloves, he got the ladder from the basement and placed it on the edge of the roof. Careful not to place the ladder on the gutters he moved it toward the end of the roof. This was where the concrete central drain for all the adjoining gutters emptied. Confident that he had calculated the measurements correctly and had determined the proper placement of the ladder, he climbed up onto the roof. His plan was to start shoveling the top of the roof working his way down to the edge of the porch roof. He had accomplished shoveling the snow off one third of the roof when his foot slipped and he was in a free fall towards the ground. Frantically he grabbed anything his hand could grasp to break his fall. The only solid thing he found was the edge of the concrete main gutter. He grabbed as much of it as he could while sliding down the pipe like a greased monkey. It was of no avail, he continued plummeting into the deep snow.

His effort was too little, too late, and he was buried face down into a huge snowdrift. When he finally realized that he was still breathing, he clawed his way out of the drift hoping he was in one piece. Satisfied that he was not broken anywhere, he got to his feet coated in fine powder snow. He was covered in snow and pellets of ice clinging to his beard. Opal was looking out the window when she noticed a flying object falling to the ground. Realizing that Mike was on the roof, she hurried out to see if the flying object was Mike.

When she saw him standing dusted from head to toe in the white powdery snow she laughed.

"Mike, you look like a gingerbread man who has been doused in powdered sugar," she cried. Her laughter caused Mike to look at himself and see how goofy he looked. He could only laugh with her as they both began to brush off the snow that was imbedded in his clothes. They went into the kitchen and while Mike removed his snowy clothes, Opal put the kettle on to make a hot cup of tea. There were cookies just out of the oven on a plate on the table and Mike helped himself to the two biggest ones. Over tea and cookies they both had a good laugh and thanked the Lord that Mike was not injured. "But I will never forget what you looked like as long as I live," Opal said when they finally quit laughing.

Turning the pages and seeing more pictures of Mike, the memory of Mike's injury while working at the mine brought a wave of sadness. He was not supposed to be at work that day. His office had called him for an emergency. He was their senior engineer and was expected to respond to any and all problems. The cause of alarm was a portion of the roof in the lower tunnel showed signs of collapse. Mike had been advised earlier of a small crack indicating signs of degeneration in the ceiling of one of the tunnels. He was concerned for the safety of the miners. He immediately donned his work clothes and rushed to the mine.

He took the lift down to where the fault was discovered. He realized the crack had widened in size. As he proceeded further into the mine, following the fault, he knew immediate evacuation was necessary. He needed to examine the extent of crack from its point of origin. Walking further into the tunnel he noticed the overhead timber structures were loosened and had begun to come apart. He now realized he and the other miners were in grave danger. Small and large boulders were loosened and were staring to tumble down around him. He made a run for the lift. He almost made it, but he was caught and pinned against the wall and the floor. He heard the cries of the others as they all realized they were trapped. Mike yelled into his radio for help. They had no idea how long it would take before help came. Four hours later the rescue team finally reached Mike and the others and they were rushed to the hospital. When Opal received the call about the disaster she went limp with fear and worry. Hurriedly she grabbed her coat and sped to the hospital

After X-rays were taken and evaluated the doctor advised Opal that Mike had suffered a broken shoulder, four cracked ribs and his left leg was broken in two places. He also had a severe concussion. His recovery would be rather long and painful, but he had survived with his life. Opal knelt beside his bed and prayed, thanking God for saving his life and asking Him for strength for the long healing journey that lay ahead. Mike remained in a coma for a week before he began to show any signs of recognizing people around him.

He began the slow painful recovery in constant pain exerting all his effort to just move and regain the use of his body. He had difficulty breathing due to the fractured ribs. His body cried out in pain. After four weeks in the hospital he was allowed to return home with instructions to exercise and strengthen his muscles. The head injury, however, had been serious and he had difficulty with memory and speech. His emotions were out of control at times and Opal had to adjust to his mood swings and angry outbursts. It was several months before he seemed to be in control, and even then, he slumped into a depression with suicidal thoughts. As the months passed he began to return to his normal self. However, the severe concussion limited his cognitive abilities. There were times he sought isolation to regroup his thoughts. It took deliberate effort to put pieces of his life that were misty and unclear back together. Little by little he was able to join the family on their outings and everyday life activities.

One such outing was a family ice skating adventure. It had been a harsh winter with cold winds hurling snow in all directions.

Temperatures dipped below freezing and the small lakes in the parks were frozen with a thick layer of ice. The day they chose to go out dawned bitter cold with a chilling wind. Mike and Opal bundled the three kids from head to toe looking and walking like stuffed rag dolls. Other families had gathered at the lake as Mike and Opal arrived. They found a snow-covered bench to sit down and put on their skates. Even Mike mustered enough courage to venture out on the ice with the kids. Opal chose to sit huddled in warm blankets and watch the activity from the shore. Someone had built a roaring fire and she relished its warmth.

Everyone was having such great fun including Mike, who was flying on his skates far from shore. Alice's dream of becoming a famous ice skater made her fearless on the ice. Finally she was free to practice her twirls and leaps; executing moves she had read about in books. While she was perfecting the splits, she slid spread-eagle on the ice, her legs going in opposite directions. The cold ice penetrated her warm wool pants giving her torso a jarring jolt. But that didn't deter her determination. Quickly regaining her balance she continued leaping and turning. Without realizing it she skated too far from the shore. After four concentrated efforts to do a series of complete turns, she lost her balance and once again fell. A bit dazed and stunned she tried to pull herself up but was unsteady. As she lay on the ice trying to regain her senses, she heard the ice crack. She then realized she had skated away from the solid frozen ice. Suddenly she was paralyzed with fear knowing she might fall through the ice and into the freezing water. She was afraid to move fearing she would break through. Her screams for help pierced the frigid air.

Mike was the first to respond to her cries and he shouted for her to remain still and not move. He quickly grabbed a blanket for something Alice could grab when he was close enough to reach her. Dropping down on his stomach, he started to cross the ice. The ice groaned beneath him. His plan was to throw the rolled end of the blanket for her to grab onto when he was close enough. Once she grabbed the blanket, he could then pull her slowly across the ice safely to him. She was starting to sink and Mike wasn't sure the ice was thick enough to support him. When the men on shore saw the situation unfolding, two of them rushed to assist Mike. They slid on their stomachs to distribute their weight as they pushed out to aid with the rescue. When they reached Mike, they grabbed his feet sliding with him as he inched toward Alice. Other men formed a human chain by grabbing the feet of those ahead and inching their way toward Mike and Alice. One man firmly anchored on the shore was prepared to pull the human chain safely back to land. When Mike was close enough to throw the blanket to Alice she was able to firmly grasp the end. As soon as Mike knew Alice had a grip on the blanket he called to man on shore to start pulling them in. Mike heard the ice groan as Alice began sliding toward him. Terror gripped him with the thought of freezing water sucking them down into an icy grave.

Mike slowly pulled Alice to himself, reassuring her and quieting her fears. After they were hauled ashore and Alice was safely in Opal's arms Mike realized how cold he was. His entire body had been stretched out on the freezing ice and he was shivering violently. Alice's trembling subsided when she was warmly wrapped in blankets. Mike quickly chose a spot next to the roaring fire and huddled close to chase the aching cold from his body. He reached out to thank each man who had given his body length to help save both Alice and him. Mike gave each one a firm handshake, adding a bear hug for thanks. Most of all they were thankful to God who had intervened in this crisis and that all were safe and together as a family.

It was after this dramatic event that Mike became listless. As Opal recalled those difficult times sorrow seemed to swallow her.

She had tried to brighten his days and create happy times for him, but often times he did not respond to her efforts. He never seemed to be able to dismiss discouragement from his thoughts and grew more and more despondent. He ~~had~~ developed pneumonia because of his sedentary lifestyle and, although he was treated with drugs, he never fully recovered. Even now tears welled up in Opal's eyes as she recalled his last days at home. She left his side only to tend to the children and to fix meals. As he slipped away he whispered in slurred words his love for her. The thought of seeing him again brought joy to her, "How long now will it be, Mike, before we can hold each other and forever be in the presence of God?" She thought to herself.

GEORGE'S ANTICS AND CLOSE CALL WITH DEATH

As Opal lingered in the reverie of those by-gone days, she failed to notice the sun had slipped low on the horizon and the air was losing its warmth. Closing the book silently, she laid the book on the table beside her, promising herself that she would return another day to enjoy those special days of her life. Picking up her coffee mug, she rose and went inside.

She hadn't heard Brenda come home. An hour later Brenda knocked on Opal's door and entered with a happy greeting. She had purchased steaks for grilling for dinner that evening. She told Opal she had also purchased fresh mushrooms and romaine to make a salad and asked her "Would you make the dressing that you used to make when we were all at home? You always had fresh ingredients from the garden for that wonderful salad and the dressing made everything taste like the salad had been sent special delivery from heaven's garden."

"Sure, if I can remember what the ingredients were. It has been a long time since I made it. I'll guess the measurements and see what turns out."

The weather was so pleasant at dinnertime they decided to eat on the patio. Eating outside was a welcome novelty for Opal. She seldom had the opportunity and a place to enjoy her meals outdoors. After dinner they lingered outside over a glass of wine while as the moon appeared on the horizon. It was a pleasant evening. As they rose to retreat inside, Opal said good night and closed her patio door. Opal got ready for bed thinking she would read for a while comfy in her robe and slippers. However, it wasn't long before her eyes became too heavy to read anymore. She closed the book, and after laying it aside on the table, she crawled into bed. The perfect evening and the glass of wine gently ushered her into the arms of sleep. It had been the best of days!

The days passed rapidly and Opal was finding her identity in this new environment fulfilling and agreeable. It was wonderful having time to leisurely page through the albums that had been untouched for years. The photos allowed her to relive the great times she had enjoyed in her life. Years ago she had set aside these albums for a later time and forgotten about them. Now they seemed to be a lifeline connecting her to who she was when she had lived in her *painted lady*. As she was turning the pages in the album, Butterscotch (nicknamed BS), Brenda's big calico cat, seized the opportunity to jump onto her lap. Settling himself into a round ball he began purring. This dear one had become a comfort to her since living here and she welcomed the cat's presence. As she continued thumbing through the photos, she recalled so many memories. They flashed across her mind overwhelming her senses with the joy and sadness that she had known.

As she flipped the pages her eye fell on the snapshot of George and Mike holding George's first fish. The two had gone fishing and George had snagged a beautiful big trout, fifteen inches long and weighing five pounds. He was beaming from ear to ear as he proudly held up his fish. That had been a special time for father and son to bond and become better acquainted. They had more outings after that special time and George brought home more big fish for supper. Even though George was still a young boy, his dad Mike took him bird hunting, with the promise of hunting his first deer as soon as he got his hunting license. He had become his father's son in many ways and they spent some evenings just sitting around a campfire talking *man things* as George labeled it

Ah, that little mischievous guy! Opal recalled how he constantly taunted the girls with his repertoire of tricks and teases. The little dickens put toothpaste on Brenda's hairbrush she always kept in the bathroom. Sneaking in late at night when the girls were in bed he squeezed a large blob of paste onto the brush, thoroughly rubbing it into the thick bristles. During the night the paste had penetrated every fiber of the brush. The next morning after Brenda took a shower and washed her hair, she picked up her brush and vigorously began brushing. White foam oozed out of the brush and into her hair and she screamed thinking she had a disease. She came running down the stairs and flung herself sobbing into Opal's arms. When Opal quieted her she noticed the foam and knew exactly what it was: George had been at it again! When Brenda realized what had happened, she grabbed the kitchen broom and chased George around the house. George was laughing hysterically as he bounded up the steps and into his room. He closed the door and locked it. He leaned his weight against the door making sure Brenda didn't come crashing through.

One particular occasion he discovered a large snail in the backyard. He brought it into the house and stashed it in his closet. When he was sure Alice was gone he tiptoed into her room and firmly placed the snail in her bedroom slipper. To be sure the critter didn't leave its hiding place, he laid her other slipper gently over the top of the shoe. The next morning when Alice got out of bed to get dressed, she slid her foot into the slipper. There was this slimy thing crunched against her toe. She let out a scream, quickly dumping her slipper upside down shaking it furiously. When she saw that icky creature she knew immediately who had done this. George! She picked up her slipper and raced into George's bedroom throwing the slipper as hard as she could in his face. He pulled the covers over his head as she started flailing him with all of her might.

Another time he placed a rubber snake under the covers in Alice's bed, for her to discover when she got ready for bed. It startled her at first, but she recognized the handiwork of one devious brother. Rather than give him the satisfaction of scaring her, she quietly put the snake in her dresser drawer and went to bed. George kept waiting for the screams of terror and when they didn't come he peeked into her room and found Alice fast asleep. He didn't know why she hadn't reacted until a day later when he finally asked her about a snake in her bed. She replied, "What snake? There was nothing in my bed so it must have crawled away." The scoreboard now read:

ALICE----1 GEORGE----0

A few days later Opal was in the kitchen mixing dough with her hands when George came into the room. He watched her for a minute or two then asked, "Mom, do you have a couple of old coffee mugs I could have? Maybe ones that we no longer use?"

Opal thought for a moment and then said, "There might be some in the very back of the cupboard. You will need to check yourself because my hands are sticky with dough. There might even be one with some flowers on it. Just look and see."

George pushed all the cups and mugs aside and reached into the back cupboard. There were three that Opal said he could have. He selected one with the faded flowers and one with colored rings around the top. The other one he replaced back into the cupboard.

"Thanks Mom, I can use these."

"What do you want those old mugs for?" Opal asked.

"I have a project in mind and I need coffee mugs." With that remark he went out the back door. Opal puzzled about what on earth he would need mugs for in a project, but she did not pursue the thought any further.

George went to the edge of the woods behind their house where he had found a patch of purple and white wild violets. Taking the trowel he had brought, he dug up clumps of violets and carefully placed some in each of the mugs. After patting the soil firmly around the plants, he achieved the effect he imagined.

Carefully he tucked both mugs under his jacket and returned home. He entered by the back door making sure no one saw him.

Silently he crept up the stairs to his room and put his treasures behind his shoes in the closet. Earlier he had gone to the drug store and bought two heart-shaped lollipops, which were safely stashed in his dresser. Satisfied that all was well hidden, he washed his hands in the bathroom and went downstairs to join the family.

When dinner was finished that evening, and while others were engaged in their own activities, George ambled up to his room on the pretense of reading a book. As the evening passed, his parents and siblings called him to join them in the living room for a game. But George was insistent that he wanted to finish the book he was reading. As the night wore on, Alice and Brenda finally decided it was time to go to bed. The parents weren't far behind. About 11:30 George peeked out from behind his bedroom door and determined the house was quiet and nobody was up. He retrieved his coffee mugs, inserted the heart shaped lollipops into each one and tiptoed into the hall. Quietly he placed a mug in front of his sister's bedroom doors and then quietly returned to his room.

Next morning everyone was slowly stirring. Brenda was the first to open her door to go to the bathroom to brush her teeth. She nearly stumbled over the flowering mug and shouted, "What is this? Why is this mug by my door? Who did this?"

Alice opened her door to see what Brenda was shouting about and discovered that she, too, had a mug by her door. She thought she knew who the mug fairy was and quietly walked around the mug of flowers to George's room. Knocking on his door and calling out to him, she opened the door and saw him sitting on the side of the bed laughing.

"I thought so," she said. "This has your signature on this trick! Why, little Brother, the pot of flowers?"

George sheepishly replied, "Treats for tricks. Guess I have been a bit too much at playing tricks, so I wanted to say I'm sorry. If I promise to be a better brother, can we be friends?"

They both broke out laughing and immediately hugged each other. Alice reassured George all was good between them.

Brenda, hearing the commotion in the hall with laughter coming from George's room came to his doorway and saw this unusual sight of brother hugging sister. She demanded to know what happened. Alice filled her in on the mug mystery and the reason behind the offerings. She, too, began to laugh and grabbed George by the shoulders and gave him a big bear hug. As they started down the stairs for breakfast, they were still giggling with the arms of all three entangled around each other.

So unusual was this sight of friendship between them that Opal wanted to know the reason for this miracle. They explained what the mystery man had done and why. Opal now knew why George wanted the coffee mugs. The morning was off to a good start with enough smiles to last all day and maybe even into the evening.

On a warm sunny May afternoon, George called his friends to ask if they would like to meet for a game of baseball at the park just outside of town. All were eager to get outside and meet for a game or two. They played most of the afternoon with such fervor and enthusiasm they collapsed on the grass for a breather. A suggestion was made to go for ice cream at the local drug store and everyone heartily agreed. The other boys left on their bikes while George stayed behind to gather the equipment, saying he would catch up with them in a short time. Putting the bats and mitts in his oversized bike basket he started toward town.

He was half way to town when a drunk driver came barreling down the street weaving erratically and headed straight toward George on his bike. The car was coming up fast behind him and George did not have time to react. The driver swerved when he spotted George, but his foggy brain did not react quickly enough. He swerved directly into George from behind. George was thrown off his bike onto the side of the road landing on his head and shoulders. The drunken driver stopped down the road and stumbled back to the scene. The shock of what just happened sobered him somewhat when he saw George lying on the ground with blood coming from his nose, mouth and head. A driver in a passing car stopped and offered what help he could, and he thought it best to call an ambulance and get him to a hospital immediately.

At the hospital the doctors quickly assessed the damage and immediately x-rayed his head and upper body to determine the extent of his injuries. The doctors were especially worried because his brain was beginning to swell. This would require close monitoring in case the swelling increased. If this occurred George would need emergency surgery to open his skull to drain excess fluid to prevent any brain damage. George was placed in ICU.

Opal was out in the backyard preparing her flowerbeds for spring planting when she heard the phone ring. She grudgingly pulled off her garden gloves, dusted off her pants and made her way to the house. The phone had rung incessantly and Opal answered with an irritated voice. Her irritation quickly changed into a scream of disbelief and terror. Fumbling for the chair beside the phone she collapsed onto it as the news penetrated her senses. When the numbness subsided she asked if George was alive. When she learned that he was alive but had serious injuries, she regained her voice in relief. She hung up the phone and immediately called Mike. He told her he was coming for her as soon as he hung up the phone. Time was of the essence as they rushed to the hospital.

When Opal and Mike arrived they saw George, his head completely bandaged, his shoulder in a cast and multiple bruises on his upper body. The doctor told them George had sustained a broken shoulder and three fractured ribs in addition to his head injuries. His body had taken a severe blow when he was hurled from his bike. The doctors were watching him to be sure he did not have any signs of internal bleeding.

Mike tried to calm Opal, who was becoming hysterical. Even though he held her close there wasn't anything he could say to negate what the doctors had described about George's condition. As they grappled for control of their anxiety they held his hands praying silently for healing and for their own peace. George was in a coma and was unable to hear his parents talking.

Two weeks later George slowly began recovering from his coma and recognizing his parents. However, he had no recollection of what happened to him and why he was in such pain. Opal shared small bits of information about the accident, stressing that it was a miracle he had survived. As George faded in and out of his never land Opal stayed by his side, constantly praying for healing his broken body. While George was being monitored closely for any long-term problems, Opal was told there could possibly be injury to his spinal cord which could hinder the complete use of his legs. This latest news lingered over them like a dark cloud as they prayed and waited. Would George fully recover and be restored to his previous robust self?

After George awoke from his coma he was in a lot of pain and needed pain killers. The doctor told his family George would need to stay in the hospital until he regained the ability to care for himself. The verdict of whether he would regain the use of his legs was still unknown. A physical therapist worked with him encouraging him to soldier through the pain and push for control of his body. Most days George was exhausted from the effort. He told Opal he was determined to get through this ordeal and return home. Learning to use his legs was his top priority and he pushed harder through the exercises the therapist gave him. He would walk again!

After four weeks in the hospital, the doctor felt that George was recovered enough to go home. He reminded George that a lot of effort would determine if he would regain the use of his legs. George returned home and Opal kept vigil over his bed as he recovered.

Many times she sensed the prayers of another mother long ago as she, too, stood by her sick child's bed. Opal felt her pain mingled with her own.

One evening as George was reclining on the living room couch, he said to his mom, "You know, Mom, during my struggles in the hospital I sometimes thought the effort of trying to regain my strength was not worth it. Discouragement shrouded my mind telling me I would never have a normal life. But in those darkest moments I had an epiphany that God was speaking to me. I felt His presence right beside me telling me I would return to normal and He had plans for my life. It was just this one time, and that time grabbed me and gave me the will and the strength to soldier on." Opal was not surprised at this revelation because she, also, felt the hand of God during those days in the hospital. "We will continue to pray God will reveal His plans for you."

After this conversation with his mother, George's mind was constantly seeking the will of God for his life. During idle times when he was unable to be active, he imagined different choices for his life. One Tuesday morning shortly after breakfast, he received a phone call from a church member asking him if would share his testimony about how God had encouraged him to persist in his rehabilitation with the youth group. George readily accepted and as he began to prepare his thoughts to share, it seemed natural to him. He knew this avenue of sharing God with others was something he enjoyed doing. A revelation dawned on him—he would enter the ministry and become a pastor.

BRENDA'S FAIRY ENCOUNTER

Brenda chose a picture-perfect day to take the day off from work so she and Opal could have lunch. Brenda suggested this special little tearoom she had recently discovered. The atmosphere was in the Victorian tradition, with lunch served on linen tablecloths and napkins and tea in antique cups and saucers. The menu of cakes, sandwiches and fruit selections was the perfect choice for an enjoyable afternoon with Opal. She anticipated a wonderful time of sharing.

Opal was thrilled with the idea of an afternoon with Brenda over tea and cakes. Brenda came by to pick her up at 2:00 and together they embarked on a delightful afternoon. Opal chose her favorite dress of delicate blue with a rolled collar of white dotted satin. She decided the occasion called for her spring hat bedecked with blue and white violets. It had been a long time since she had been excited about anything. When Brenda opened the door, she saw Opal's smile radiating like a morning sunrise.

The tearoom was a delight. The windows with their lace-ruffled valances overlooked a garden filled with flowers and blooming shrubs. They chose a table next to a window and ordered lavender and mint tea---the owner's favorite. Brenda chose an assortment of teacakes and scones to accompany their tea. They were seated and served. As they nibbled on scones and sipped tea, Brenda asked Opal if she had made a decision about the remaining things left in storage. "Not really" Opal replied. "I have been enjoying my new life here so much and the past is just a memory of happy times. You might want to take inventory and see if there are things that are meaningful to you and choose something for yourself."

"I am so glad that you are satisfied and content with us. You are focusing on your future and keeping your past like pleasant jewels of memories to revive and relive them as you choose." The afternoon passed pleasantly as they talked about Opal's arrival and how quickly she was settling into her new lifestyle.

As they chatted and laughed over things of the past, Opal asked if Brenda remembered the time she had German measles.

"Oh yes, even though it was a painful time it also was a special time. Do you remember when I discovered the box of stories and sketches in Jennifer's closet? I found them when I was searching for my lost scarf. They had been hidden on the top shelf in the closet. She had written fairy stories with sketches. After reading the stories, I put them back and forgot about them. It was when I was sick with the German measles those stories literally came to life. Did I ever tell you about my experience during that time? It warms my heart in just telling about it. It was another *whispering* of the past echoing in our grand old house."

Opal said, "I don't recall any story; only how very sick and uncomfortable you were. Tell me about your experience."

Brenda began. "I wasn't feeling well as I left for school one windy March morning. By the time recess arrived, I asked to stay inside instead of going out to play. By lunchtime I was feverish and a bit nauseous. I asked if I could go home. After arriving home, I immediately told you I felt very ill and wanted to go straight to bed. Slipping into my pajamas, I wasted no time crawling beneath the covers. You immediately checked my temperature, concerned when it was 103.4 and you called the doctor listing my symptoms. The doctor asked if I had flushed skin and if I had red spots beginning to rise on my arms, neck and torso. When you answered affirmatively to his questions, his diagnosis was measles, and most probably German measles. He advised you to watch over me for the next twenty-four hours observing if the red spots became more numerous and if they were increasingly red and blotchy. A cool soda bath helped to cool my fever and calm any itching. My temp dropped two degrees and I fell into a fitful sleep.

The fairies hiding in Jennifer's box heard my pitiful cries of discomfort as I lay in bed covered with red blotches. Immediately they gathered together and flew to my bedside. Hovering over me, they gently touched my head and nose, whispering encouragement and quiet songs of love. My body began to relax and a smile appeared on my face. The nymphs stayed close by through the night, and if I stirred, they quickly flew to my side reassuring me with their whispers of love. I was on my way to healing.

Two nights later, I felt a tickling sensation on my nose and ear. I swiped at what I thought was a fly but the feeling did not go away. Tiny squeaks of laughter hovered above my ear followed by the giggling of small creatures. I thought my dreams were coming alive and turned over in bed to escape from my imagination. However, the tinkling noises did not cease. I sat up in bed and was amazed to see tiny creatures flying above my head. My first thought was that they were fireflies, but they are seldom seen indoors. Still confused by what I was seeing, I just sat spellbound and listened.

The tiny voices whispered in my ear that they came to cheer me and make me well. They told me they had a story to tell me and it would make me feel better. They instructed me to lie back down, listen and let their story fill me with happy thoughts. This was the story they told:

A girl was strolling in a field of daisies, running her hands over the mass of flowers. She stopped at one big blossom, deciding it was the perfect daisy she was seeking. The white petals extending from the golden center appeared like ribbons framing the happy face of the flower. She knew this was the one that would tell her if her boyfriend liked her. Carefully plucking the blossom, she sniffed for its fragrance and then pulled one of the petals saying "he loves me, he loves me not".

The daisy cried out "Ouch! That hurt! What are you doing to me?"

Ignoring the daisy's cry, the girl pulled another petal repeating," he

loves me, he loves me not". The daisy quickly became a bit ragged and cried out again "Stop that!"

Hearing the daisy's cry, the girl stopped pulling the petals, considering whether to continue or to just discard the whole flower. The daisy was screaming and gathering all the remaining petals into her heart, asked "Why is my body being torn apart?" This caught the girl's attention and looking down at the tattered flower, she said "Sorry, I didn't realize I was hurting you. I am trying to determine if my boyfriend loves me or not and using your petals will tell me his feelings."

The daisy began to relax her petals allowing them to extend fully. "Of course, he loves you. I could have told you this if you had just asked me, and I wouldn't be in this ragged condition. Of course he loves you. There is no reason he wouldn't love you. You are so pretty and you are kind to people and animals, but not to daisies. Since you now know the answer, could you please stop pulling any more of my petals?"

The girl released her fingers from the petals, asking if she could take her home and place her in a tiny vase where her beauty would remind her of her boyfriend's love. The daisy was all too happy to be carried home and placed in a vase of water where she could live out the rest of her life. Everyone was happy.

The fairies told me, if you are kind to people and animals your life will go well. They assured me that I was a kind person and someday soon, I would get well and kindness would follow me the rest of my life.

I fell into a peaceful sleep while my body continued its healing journey. I felt restored."

AUSTIN AND ALICE

Brenda finished the story and they sat quietly reflecting. They chatted for a while and then Brenda asked, "Have you heard from Alice recently?" Recollections of Alice's unhappy marriage to Austin flashed across Opal's mind.

"No, after she came home to escape Austin, she took time to settle her thoughts. She decided to take a nursing position as far away as possible from Austin. She is so afraid Austin will track and find her. From time to time, she calls assuring me she is okay, but chooses to keep her location secret. He did, in fact, call harassing me seeking her location. I told him she had no permanent address. It is such a sad situation and I miss having contact with her, and I can understand her cause for concern."

"She went through such a terrible experience with Austin and I wonder if she will ever be able to trust men again!", Brenda added.

This conversation opened up painful memories of Alice's brush with death. Alice had gone to college at the university in Missoula to train as a nurse. She was brilliant and quickly rose to the top of her class. The family was happy she had found her purpose in life and was embracing it with gusto. She met Austin in her junior year and they seemed to be a perfect couple. Austin was studying physical education, planning to teach and coach high school students. After graduating and dating only a year, they became engaged. When Alice brought Austin home during the last year of school, the family found it was difficult to engage him in conversation about his family and background. Even starry-eyed Alice didn't know much about Austin's background.

After graduation Austin found a job teaching in Whitefish, Montana and the couple settled into a small apartment. Alice found a job in a doctor's office as a nurse and doctor's assistant. They were deliriously happy for the first six months. They went skiing, hiking in the beautiful mountains, and life seemed so perfect. On one occasion, however, when Alice was late coming home from her job, Austin met her at the door with fury in his eyes demanding to know where she had been and who she had been with. Alice quickly assured him it was an emergency at the office and the doctor had gotten behind seeing his scheduled patients. She had stayed late to assist him. Austin calmed down and apologized for his outburst.

Later that evening after dinner Austin told Alice his controlling mother caused his father to rebel and, over time, become violent. As a young child Austin had witnessed his parents in heated arguments and, in some cases, physical confrontation.

"I learned to escape from the violence by retreating to my room and closing the door. Sometimes my father failed to bring his anger under control and I witnessed him banging my mother's head against the wall. When I tried to intervene, I was quickly shoved aside, threatened and told to leave. I can still hear my parents' shouting threats and vile accusations at each other."

Alice was so surprised and saddened to hear Austin's childhood history. "I had no idea that you had such a painful childhood with no one to support you. It must have been traumatic witnessing horrific fights between your parents. Your sharing this helps me understand how I can support you, reassuring you of my love."

Their conversation was now couched in loving words with encouragement. Alice put her arms around Austin reassuring him he was loved and safe with her. The rest of the evening was spent watching TV curled up together on the sofa. They went to bed hand in hand and Alice felt a closeness to Austin that she had not felt before.

Things were normal for the next few weeks and life returned to their daily routines. Austin began to experience some difficulty with his students in class and in his coaching. He demanded perfection to the point that his students were becoming frustrated, and resentful and fearful of him. Several times his anger erupted and he was at the point of almost attacking a student. He struggled with the desire to strike out when they did not please him. He felt helpless to control his constant pent up anger. This constant fury took its toll on him. It left him edgy and uncommunicative with Alice. She, in turn, reasoned that all of his actions at home were due to his fractured background and she let his caustic words go unchallenged.

As time went on, he criticized her for trivial things and made extreme issues out of small incidents. Alice continued to ignore most of this but when Austin started to throw small things causing them to break, she realized this was a different phase that she did not appreciate and was not going to tolerate. When she confronted him he yelled and belittled her with accusatory words. As his behavior continued and he refused to talk about his actions, Alice frequently worked late at the office to avoid being around Austin and having to deal with his attitude and actions. It wasn't long before Austin became suspicious because Alice came home late. He began to grill her about her whereabouts as soon as she came home from work. Even though she patiently explained she was at work, and had come straight home after work, he still accused her of going out with friends instead of coming home. His outbursts became outrageous and Austin demanded Alice quit her job and stay home to be a dutiful wife. At this point she had all she could take and was through trying to appease him.

This was the last straw for Alice. She demanded they seek a marriage counselor to help them work through Austin's anger problem and the crisis it was causing in their marriage. Austin agreed to give counseling a try, but he held no hope for any solution because he was convinced that Alice was unwilling to change to meet what he thought were his legitimate requests to be the faithful wife.

Early the next morning Alice was up and preparing breakfast as usual. Austin joined her and they ate in stony silence. Alice cleared and washed the dishes, setting them in the rack to dry. She went into the bathroom to get ready for work while Austin dressed and left for school. When Alice was sure he had left, she packed a few things. Picking up her purse she reached for her car keys in the usual spot on the hall table where she always left them. But they were not there! Confused, she thought back to when she had used them last. She was certain she had left them where she always did when she arrived home. They just weren't there. She searched in her purse, the pockets of her sweater, even looking through the window of her car thinking she might have left them there. They were nowhere to be found. Then she thought maybe Austin had picked up her keys mistakenly thinking that he had gotten his keys. But his keys were also gone. Then she realized he had deliberately taken her keys to keep her from leaving. She couldn't reach him until he was out of his class, so she left a message to call her. When he called he apologized for taking her keys. His excuse was he wanted to have her oil and brake fluid checked. He volunteered to come home and take her to work between his classes.

She told him that would not be necessary. She had decided she wasn't going to work anyway and would call in sick. Instead she called a taxi to take her to the bus station planning to take the first bus to Helena. Picking up her purse she had a feeling she should check to see if she had enough money to pay for the taxi and bus fare. There was no money in her wallet and her credit card was gone. Austin had completely stolen every bit of value from her purse. She then realized he was trying to take control of her and she needed to do something soon to protect her independence and sanity.

Lying in bed that night, Alice began planning how to deal with Austin's new level of controlling behavior. After much consideration, she felt her best plan was to remain calm and not question the reasons behind his behavior. This would take extreme caution in choosing her words and how she responded to his intense suspicion, accompanied by his need to control her every move. But she must not allow him to reach the point where he became mentally and physically threatening. She decided to consult with her doctor when she returned to work.

The following morning after the disappearance of her car keys and her credit cards, she greeted Austin with a cheerful "Morning" as she prepared breakfast. Austin seemed calmer and like his old self, so she ventured to raise the issue of the missing car keys.

"Honey, the next time you want to take my car to be checked for any problems, would you let me know so I can make arrangements to go to work later, or have one of my friends give me a ride?"

With a mouthful of toast, Austin replied, "Sure, and I'll let you know when I take your car for any reason. My main concern is to make sure the car is safe for you to drive."

After breakfast, they each started getting ready for the day. Alice stayed a little longer after Austin left to be sure that he was gone and not waiting for her. After she determined that the coast was clear she started for her car. Out of the corner of her eye she spotted Austin's car parked a block away around the corner from their apartment building. She pretended she didn't see him and proceeded to get into the car. As she drove off she kept glancing at her rear view mirror to see if Austin was behind her. He was! She continued on her way as though everything was normal.

When she reached her office, she did not show any signs of signs of having seen Austin. She glanced through the office window and saw he had disappeared down the street. Her first instinct was to talk to her doctor about how to handle this new situation. However, she thought better of it because the fewer people that knew about her concerns, the less risk there would be for someone to say something that might get back to Austin. The rest of the day was a routine one. She deliberately stayed a little bit after the last appointment, and after everyone had gone home. She watched out the window (out of sight of anyone outside) and waited to see if Austin would be somewhere waiting for her to leave. And he was! He was parked behind several other cars across the street in the parking lot of a shopping mall. He had slid down in the seat thinking he would not be noticed, but Alice was aware of his presence. She went to her car and on her way home she stopped at the grocery store for some items and then proceeded home. She had not noticed him following her and was surprised when he was at the door to greet her when she walked from the garage.

By this time Alice had decided that the best way to handle Austin's actions was to act as though everything was normal between them. She felt that by her not antagonizing him with questions, he would relax and she could get a better feel about what her next step of action would be.

Things continued as normal for the next few weeks. Austin seemed lost in his work and Alice sensed that he longer felt threatened by her absence. However, one Thursday after he came home from coaching a ball game Alice was not home. She had accepted an invitation from a friend in her Yoga class to have a late lunch. She was having such a good time and enjoying being free from Austin's demands she forgot about Austin's requirement that she be home when he got back form his school's games.

She arrived home smiling and in a happy mood, and it was obvious to Austin that she had been somewhere other than work. He was furious and greeted her when she came in with a burst of demands regarding her whereabouts. Before she could tell him about her afternoon with a lady friend, he began shouting at her and using foul language. She had never seen him like this and it frightened her. She gave him time to exhaust his angry outburst and then asked if they could sit down and discuss this without shouting. But Austin wasn't through and he reacted to her quiet demeanor and soft answer by shaking her by the shoulders and threatening her, telling her she was never to go anywhere unless she asked him first.

This was a new unnerving development and Alice retreated to their bedroom locking the door behind her. Austin knocked chairs over and stomped through the house, fuming and muttering threats.

There was no dinner that night and Alice did not come out of the bedroom. When Austin finally calmed down, he took a shower and then knocked on the door telling her he was sorry for his actions. He begged her to come out and listen to him. He wanted to apologize. She felt that if she didn't try to make some kind of peace with him, he might fly into another rage and become violent with her again. She slowly opened the door and they stood there facing each other.

Alice said, "Austin, I cannot live with you shaking me to vent your anger. This must never happen again and I need you to promise me that you won't ever reach out to me in anger. This is not an indication of love. I don't want to live in fear of you."

Austin promised it would never happen again and apologized again for shaking her. Alice went back into the bedroom, gathered a pillow and a blanket, and got her toothbrush and a change of clothes. She left the room and hung her clothes in the hall closet. Putting her bedding on the couch she announced she would spend the night there. Austin was sullen and pouted, but Alice made no more conversation and virtually ignored him for the rest of evening.

The following morning was ice cold between them as Alice made sandwiches for their lunches and got ready for work. During the night She decided she would call the organization that could advise her about what to do or where to go. She would continue to research her options and set a goal to escape when the occasion arose.

The results of her search disclosed a local group against violence towards women met in a nearby community center. She made plans to attend. The meeting was held on Thursdays evenings from 7:00–8:30. She was warned she should not share any information with her husband about her attending the meetings. Alice spoke to her doctor about claiming Thursday evenings as a work late night. If Austin was checking up on her whereabouts, he could confirm the new arrangement with her doctor. She felt sure Austin would check to verify she was telling the truth. She would leave and return through the back door, leave a light on in the office and go to the meeting. After the meeting she would return to the office and turn off the lights. Her doctor would confirm her alibi by saying that he had reserved Thursday evenings for people who worked during the day and could not come for appointments during regular office hours.

Alice was confident Austin would hold her accountable. She shared the news about the doctor being open on Thursday evenings with Austin, thereby making it necessary to be at work during dinnertime. Austin didn't challenge this information but he wanted to know the exact time the office closed. She knew he would check to validate she was telling him the truth. And he did! The next day he strolled into the office after the last patient left and told Alice they were going out to dinner. He waited while Alice changed from her uniform into her street clothes and he walked into the doctor's office. The doctor was one step ahead of him and when he greeted Austin, the doctor voiced his concerns that keeping Alice late on Thursday evenings would inconvenience Austin. Austin sheepishly agreed that it would be fine.

The first Thursday was a little shaky for Alice. She felt like she was on a secret mission, fearful Austin would discover her deceit. After three weeks she began to feel this whole process would work out. A few times Austin did go by the office checking to be sure Alice was working. Seeing the light on in the office assured him that it was business as usual.

Austin began to theorize in his troubled mind that Alice was having an affair with the doctor. The more he thought about it the more enraged he became. On the third Thursday when Alice came home, he was waiting for her with fists clenched and fury boiling out of him. She put her things on the table and Austin started with his accusations, his voice rising with each threat. Alice had never seen him like this and it frightened her. She loudly denied any affair but he would not be consoled. With a burst of anger he struck her across her face. She screamed and that infuriated him even more. He grabbed her shoulders and shook her violently, slamming her against the wall. She cried out in pain and pleaded with him to stop, but he hit her head against the wall until she lost consciousness.

Her screams did not go unnoticed. A gentleman walking on the sidewalk outside saw Austin leave. He then hurried up the steps and went inside to find Alice bleeding and moaning in pain. He quickly dialed 911 and waited until the ambulance arrived. The paramedics stabilized Alice and put her into the ambulance. The gentleman chose to go with her to the hospital. Alice needed several stitches on her head. She suffered a concussion along with bruises and painful rib fractures. The gentleman stayed with her until she regained consciousness and the police arrived. When the police had taken her report of the attack, Alice reached out to the gentleman and grasped his hand. Though she could barely speak she thanked him for saving her life and asked his name. He kissed her hand and told her he was the one who had been at the right place at the right time and was there by God's providence. Then he was gone.

As she was recovering, Alice tried the find the stranger. No one remembered anyone being with her or staying with her at the hospital. She began to wonder if her mind had played tricks on her since no one had any idea who she was talking about. Lying in the hospital bed she began to recount all that had happened and slowly it dawned on her; the gentleman was an angel sent by God to care for her. Now she knew without any doubt the gentleman was an angel sent to save her. That realization changed her life forever.

At Alice's request a restraining order was issued against Austin. Alice knew that as soon as she was dismissed from the hospital Austin would arrive at her door. As soon as she was well enough to travel, she made arrangements to fly to her mother in Helena. Information about her destination must not be shared with anyone. She would recover at home and make plans to get lost from Austin.

Her doctor came to see Alice while she was in the hospital. He suggested a possible opportunity as a traveling nurse. Austin would never find her. The idea of applying for a nursing position aboard the Mercy Ship really appealed to Alice. The ship would be in port at different world-wide locations. In the remote case Austin traced her, she would have protection from the authorities on board the ship. The doctor helped her fill out the paper work and contact the proper channels to get the ball rolling. She was safe at her mother's home until she was hired and became a full time resident on board the ship. It seemed her angel did more than save her life; he guided her to a safe, new and exciting life.

Alice flew home the day after her dismissal from the hospital. It was so comforting to be under her mom's loving care and safety of her home. Slowly she gained back her strength and some of the bruising on her body became less painful. She and Opal spent many hours recalling times from the past when everybody was home and life seemed normal. Her heart ached to have that wonderful life back again. She shared her plans with Opal about being a nurse on the Mercy Ship. Now it was more than an escape from Austin, it was an opportunity to pay back the goodness shown her by the stranger who saved her life.

Austin was served with a restraining order with the promise of jail if he violated the order. He was also on probation at his school job. It seemed that he had finally realized he was no longer in control of anyone; least of all himself.

Alice received a letter for a position interview with the Mercy

Ship doctors. She made plans to fly to New York for the interview. She was excited and although Opal was excited for her, she knew she would see Alice even less than she had when Alice was working in Whitefish. They discussed plans in case Austin discovered where she had been staying, and what Opal could truthfully tell him. She truly didn't know where Alice could be reached. Alice would be the one to contact Opal after she was hired. Alice, however, would not disclose her location.

Alice went for the interview and was offered a position as a full-time nurse with the company. They were interested in training her on-the-job as a surgical nurse, with the hopes that she would be fully qualified and able to travel full time as the ship moved from one port to another. She accepted and she was told to report the following Monday. She had a week to become acquainted with the procedures, environment and requirements for her nursing duties. Before she actually set sail she met with the doctors and other nursing staff and settled into her quarters. The ship was scheduled to set sail four weeks from the time Alice came onboard.

Alice was so excited and could hardly wait until she got home to tell Opal about her new life. It was bitter sweet for Opal because she didn't know when she would see Alice again. Certainly she was happy for this wonderful new opportunity for Alice, but the uncertainty of not ever knowing Alice's whereabouts sent a cold shiver down her back. Alice would be out of Austin's reach and that was the greatest relief that Opal felt.

Alice flew home to spend the last two days with Opal before she was scheduled to return for duty. They enjoyed walking around the neighborhood reminiscing about the days when Alice was a child. They laughed about Alice losing her way on her first solo drive in Opal's stick shift car. The time Opal put salt in the cake batter instead of sugar. They had Jell-O for dessert that night instead of cake. The memories came spilling out and they laughed all the way home. It was a beautiful time.

At the airport Alice and Opal clung together, reluctant to separate knowing it could be an undermined time before they could be together again. One big hug and Alice tore herself away and fled to the airplane with tears spilling down her cheeks. Opal thought her heart would break when Alice turned for one last look at her mother.

The plan proved to be a very wise decision. Shortly after Alice's departure, Austin began to search for her in earnest. Her mother's house was the first place he went. Opal was honest in saying she did not know where Alice was. Alice never had the same address. She also told Austin that any correspondence she received from Alice had different postmarks. She reiterated firmly she had NO information to give him. Disgruntled, Austin stomped off with nowhere to find Alice.

THE REBIRTH OF THE PAINTED LADY

TOM AND TRICIA

Tricia was eager to get started remodeling her new home. She and Tom walked into the house early Monday morning with plans in hand eager to turn this grand Painted Lady into their dream home. Tom was searching for any structural problems. Tricia went to the kitchen and began drawing up ideas for a big efficient family kitchen. She envisioned large windows over the sink to replace the small narrow ones. The entire kitchen would need to be enlarged to make room for an island with a sink and cupboards for storing cookware. A small closet in the back of the kitchen would become a large pantry. A modern gas stove, dishwasher and built-in refrigerator would complete the efficiency of the kitchen. Both of them were aspiring chefs and loved experimenting with exotic recipes. Her dream kitchen was at her fingertips.

Tom was checking the structure upstairs where they wanted

to take out one bedroom wall to enlarge the master bedroom. They would add an adjoining spa-like bath. He needed to have measurements in mind when they contacted the construction company to explain what they wanted to change. From there he went to the basement to examine the wiring and the heating ducts. They were installing a gas line for the new gas furnace and gas fireplaces.

The house seemed to be solid and tight. Tom wanted to be sure there was enough insulation to prevent airconditioned air and heated air from escaping through loosely connected ducts. He would hire someone to be sure these things were checked and corrected. He made his way upstairs to find Tricia sketching out plans for changes to the rooms on the first floor.

They stopped at noontime and left for a quick lunch at the Mexican restaurant in town. They were so engrossed in their ideas they started talking all at once. Tricia held up her hand and stopped the chatter so they could catch their breath and eat their lunch. At the close of the day they were weary and mentally exhausted to do any more than take a hot shower and collapse into bed. This routine continued for the next week. Both of them met with the contractors and other specialists who would turn their plans into reality. It was a month before the remodeling was finished and they were able to move in and start the decorating: this was Tricia's field of expertise!

Color schemes were planned and fell into place. The home was taking on the new owner's personalities and it was beautiful. More finishing touches were being added daily and, three months after they took possession, the home was a showplace inside. They needed to concentrate on the colors for painting the exterior; colors that would reflect the beauty of this Painted Lady. Tricia went back to the library to review the style and colors used when the house was built. She then took her color wheel and plotted the colors to bring this beautiful lady to her full grandeur. After searching for names of different organizations, she found companies that specialized in restoration of homes of antiquity. She found the name of a company that specialized in restoration of regal homes built in the late 1800's. She made an appointment with the company historian to discuss the color scheme appropriate for the original Queen Anne style home. Searching through endless color combinations, Tricia finally picked four sets of colors to take home and consider.

The more she poured over the color choices, the more confused she became. She just set aside the whole choosing procedure deciding that a fresh start tomorrow would be the best plan. Her head was buzzing with all she had seen that afternoon. She asked Tom to bring a bottle of sweet wine from the fridge with two glasses and come sit with her. No conversations or possible solutions regarding color schemes were discussed as they sipped iced wine, savoring the moment of quietness and the intoxicating effect of the wine.

Then Tricia broke the silence sharing the results of her visit with the restoration company. She showed Tom the samples asking his opinion but stating no decision would be made until tomorrow when their minds were clear. With a fresh look in the morning they could choose what colors would be best. They refilled their glasses and sat back enjoying being together. Tricia wondered to herself if this was becoming more of an effort than her ability could solve?

After another glass of wine, Tricia felt composed and more in control of her ability to make proper choices; but that would be tomorrow, not now. They spent the rest of the evening on the front porch sipping wine in the glow of the mauve and blue twilight rays. A beautiful peace settled in on them both. They talked about how much had been achieved for the interior remodeling and decorating. It was encouraging to realize how far they had come. They now had a fresh enthusiasm for what lay ahead to complete their dream. They finally left the magic of the evening and headed into the house to crawl into bed.

The following week Tricia and Tom reached a decision about

paint colors, and made an appointment with the restoration company. They chose taupe, dark blue-green, cream and brick red. The major house painting job was assigned to the company. Tricia, however, wanted to paint the intricate ginger bread trim herself. This would give her the satisfaction of contributing her own talents to finishing the house she had grown to love. This endeavor took the rest of the summer and caused her lots of back and shoulder aches. She labored continuously painting tiny railings, and the framework around the windows and doors. The tupelo high on the top of the roof was the most challenging and risky, but she never tired of the exacting and tedious painting. This became an artist's canvas before her that unfolded after each piece of work was finished, bringing the beauty into focus. She was excited to see the picture coming to life with her artistic strokes.

She planned to use the turret as a mini-library. The windows allowed the daylight to flood the entire area. There was a comfortable window seat filled with soft bright colored pillows where she could retreat from her daily life to read, mediate and revel in the quiet peace it afforded. These moments would have to wait until winter when the weather no longer allowed her to paint outside. Each day she set a goal for how much painting she wanted to finish and usually she couldn't quit when she reached that goal. It was so exciting seeing the results she couldn't lay her brushes aside. She just wanted to continue on and do more.

There were many days like this for Tricia. In the meantime Tom began landscaping the large back yard. Of course, Tricia wanted flowers everywhere when she looked out her newly installed kitchen window. Tom could never quite understand this woman's love of color and flowers, but he happily complied with her wishes and was never disappointed with the results of her ideas. Her touch was obvious in her choice of brilliant colors.

They were working making flowerbeds on a June afternoon,

clearing overgrown bushes and weeds when they noticed a flat stone marker. It was covered with grass and encroaching moss. It had been obviously hidden from daylight for many years. It took a bit of digging and scraping and they discovered it was a gravestone marker for the great dog Hansel. He had been the Gross family's beloved pet. Tom continued to dig away the dirt and moss and they saw the inscription on the stone: *The Bravest and Best Friend In The Whole World*. A wave of sadness crept over them as they thought of the grief of losing a much-loved pet

By fall the weather was no longer conducive for painting outside. They returned to indoor projects inside the house. The one thing they did from the first was to remove a wall between the master bedroom and an adjoining bedroom to make an extra large master bedroom with adjoining spa and bath. It had a large glass enclosed shower where they could enjoy a steaming hot shower with ample room to sit on the shower seat and enjoy the effects the soothing effects of a steam room. This would be their retreat after working hard all day. This steamy retreat would be a lifesaver for the aches and sore muscles they acquired during their day.

Tom needed to spend more time at his job and less time with the projects at home. Tricia set to work designing color schemes for the remainder of the unfinished rooms in the house. Even though the kitchen was remodeled and a large window installed facing the backyard, the walls still needed a final coat of honey-yellow paint. The mini blinds had not yet been installed. She was pleased with the total look of warm honey toned pine cabinets, ceramic flooring with tiny dots of brown, tan and yellow, flecked with bits of gold. The harvest gold appliances blended with the warm atmosphere. The kitchen island had it's own sink and storage for cookware. Tom and Tricia were aspiring chefs and loved to experiment with new exotic recipes. Tricia knew she would spend a lot of time in this warm and sunny place.

One dreary rainy morning in October, Tricia decided to see what could be done with the uppermost floor used for a children's play room. Donning jeans and a sweatshirt, she tied her hair back with a scarf and headed upstairs intending to do housecleaning. She began straightening up the shelves. When she opened the closet door and started to arrange the things stuffed inside, she came across a little tin box with toy soldiers and a little book written by Eugene Fields. Curious, she sat down and opened the book and was so touched by the poem called *Little Boy Blue*. She wondered who and why someone put the book and box in this out of the way closet. She read the poem again, this time more slowly, absorbing the sad message.

LITTLE BOY BLUE

The little toy dog is covered with dust,
but sturdy and stanch he stands;

And the little toy soldier is red with rust.
And his musket molds in his hands.

Time was when the little toy dog was
new, and the soldier was passing fair;

And that was the time that our Little Boy
Blue kissed them and put them there.

"Now don't you go till I come". he said,
"and don't you make any noise!"

So, toddling off to his trundle bed,
he dreamt of the pretty toys.

And, as he was dreaming, an angel song
awakened our Little Boy Blue.

Oh, the years are many, the years are long,
but the little toy friends are true!

Ay, faithful to Little Boy Blue they
stand, each in the same old place

Awaiting the touch of a little hand,
the smile of a little face;

And they wonder, as waiting the long years
through in the dust of that little chair,

What has become of our Little Boy Blue,
since he kissed them and put them there?

Tricia was so overcome with emotion that tears formed in her eyes. She had to find the history of the box of toy soldiers and what little boy had once played with them. Her good intentions of cleaning were put aside and she went downstairs, changed her clothes and went to the library to continue searching the history of the house and the families who lived there. She pulled down records of people living in the house from the Humphreys family until Opal's occupation. What she found was so sad.

Earnest Gross, the oldest son, remained in the home after his parents died. His siblings married and moved away. Earnest and his wife, Carol, raised one son and one daughter. The daughter, Annette, had two boys who used the upper most room as a play area. Scottie developed scarlet fever when he was eight years old and died from complications two months later. Scottie's grandfather purchased the set of toy soldiers for him while he was so sick. Upon his death his parents put aside the box and book so that they would only be his forever. No other little hands would arrange them in play-action. It was a memorial to Scottie.

As the little lad's condition continued to worsen, he became weak and listless. His mother kept a bedside vigil. When he became so weak he could only whisper, she lay down on the bed beside him and cradled his head in her arms. She held him close praying softly. He suddenly looked up at her with his bright eyes, and spoke for the first time in days. With a faltering whisper he said, "I have to go now, Mommie. Jesus is waiting, I love you." With those words he relaxed in her arms and with an angelic smile, he slipped into the waiting arms of Jesus. Holding him close with her face pressed against his she held him tightly and with tears streaming down her face, whispered her farewell.

Tricia was beginning to hear and sense the presence of the previous years, the happy times and their tearful times. The house became a memory book written with the tears and joys of those who lived before. The Painted Lady had become a sacred place. She decided the upper room would remain as it had been for many years and she would not rearrange anything. She closed the door to the room. As she made her way down the stairs, she determined she did not want to invade the precious generation's privacy.

On an early spring morning, Tricia decided it was time to tackle the turret library room and finish the decorating she started a month earlier. Cleaning around the baseboards she discovered a small opening in the wall about a foot in length. She thought perhaps a mouse had made a nest there. She reached in and found some papers. Curious, she gently pulled until a small bound package of letters appeared. They were browned with age and upon closer inspection she saw they were love letters from Brenda's beau. There were no return addresses on the envelopes. Tricia unfolded one of the letters and realized, after reading a few sentences, they were personal. She did not want to read the emotions written in secret. She carefully placed them in a box with the intention of sending them to Opal.

She knew little or nothing about Brenda's life other than meeting her with Opal when they closed the deal on the house. She thought Brenda might feel violated if Tricia read the letters, and she wanted to respect Brenda's privacy.

THE WHISPERINGS BEGIN

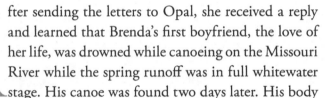

fter sending the letters to Opal, she received a reply and learned that Brenda's first boyfriend, the love of her life, was drowned while canoeing on the Missouri River while the spring runoff was in full whitewater stage. His canoe was found two days later. His body was recovered much further down the river two weeks later. Brenda was heartbroken! It was a full year before she finally reconciled to the fact he was gone. There was a pall of sadness that hung over the household as a result of her loss.

Tricia found herself emotionally drained and exhausted. She attributed the fatigue to her research of the previous owner's history. Many nights she would crawl into bed before Tom and immediately fall into a deep restless sleep. Tom was concerned but Tricia reassured him that she would feel better in the next few days.

One night around midnight Tricia was, for no reason, suddenly wide-awake. She lay in bed concentrating on returning back to sleep, but her mind was alert and listening for something. Frustrated and unable to go back to sleep, she got up and started down the stairs to the kitchen for a cup of hot chocolate. She heard what she thought were soft whispers coming from one of the other bedrooms on the second floor. Thinking she was still half asleep and possibly dreaming, she stopped at the top of the stairs and listened intently. She thought she heard a mother singing soft lullabies to a child, or perhaps praying for a child. The hair on the back of her neck stood up. She was transfixed on the spot, not sure what was happening. Suddenly the whispers ceased and Tricia thought for sure she had imagined the whole episode. She hurried down the stairs and made herself a very strong cup of hot chocolate. She slowly sipped the hot liquid while trying to make sense of what she thought she just experienced. The hot chocolate seemed to give her a sense of reality. Did she really hear the whispering? She drank the last bit of the hot cocoa, washed her cup and started back to bed. When she reached the top of the stairs, she briefly paused by the room where she heard those ethereal sounds. Determined to set her mind at ease, she peeked into the room noting that all was quiet and undisturbed. She returned to bed, but even after she was comfortable, those whispering sounds surrounded her. She finally fell into a fitful sleep. She was not ready to discuss her experience with anyone until she had some rational explanation.

As the days pasted and she had not heard or seen anything else in the house, she began to think that her mind was playing tricks on her. Her confidence was restored. She was not crazy! She made her way to one of the bedrooms on the second floor to clean the windows and give the furniture a thorough dusting. This cleaning project had been on her mind but she had not gotten to it. She was busy dusting and humming a song as she vigorously dusted the furniture. She paused for a moment. She suddenly felt she was being watched. Looking around the room she saw no one so she ignored the feeling and went to the windows to wash them. Suddenly the walls seemed to vibrate with sorrow and sobbing. A mist fell around her and she started to cry. She wanted to run from the room, but her feet felt frozen to the floor. Frantically trying to make sense of what was happening, she remembered she was in Brenda's old bedroom. Now she knew what the sorrowful atmosphere was about: it was Brenda's mourning over the loss of her lover. Realizing the reason for what was happening to her, Tricia relaxed and quietly stepped out of the room.

Once out of the room she quickly fled to the kitchen, got a wine glass and poured herself a full glass of burgundy wine. She sat down in the first chair she found and took a big draught of the wine. Several more sips brought her around to her senses. She began to think she now understood what the house was trying to tell her. So many events and emotions from *the lives of the former residents lingered within these walls. They would forever be present* to mingle and mix with the lives of the newcomers making it a forever record of the living history of this regal Painted Lady. She and Tom were just the next chapter! She began to have a new outlook and prospective about what she was experiencing in this house.

It was a busy morning and Tricia was in the kitchen making plans for dinner that evening. A slight headache was starting to give her pain, but she continued on with what she was doing. By lunchtime the pain had increased dramatically and she recognized that she had the beginning of a migraine. Having experienced these headaches before, she knew the only way to abort a more serious onslaught was to take medication her doctor had prescribed the last time this occurred. She called the pharmacy and asked for a refill. Unfortunately, they would have to call her physician to renew the medication. When the pharmacy called to tell her the prescription was ready, she called Tom and asked if he could bring it home when he had a break in his workday.

The best way to wait until Tom brought home the medicine was to stretch out on the couch with a cluster of pillows and a light blanket. The pain continued to increase as she fetched a blanket and arranged the pillows. Snuggling down she waited for relief to come! Staying as quite as she could and trying to relax to keep the pain from increasing, she lay there immobile. It was then she thought she heard a few faint lines from a song.... *this little light......let it shine.......can't put out..........this little l i g h t.......* This was a song she knew. Where had she heard this before?? Then she remembered from her research the second lady of this house held Bible classes for her neighborhood children. This was a whispering from the past. She allowed the soothing words and the sound of children's voices to quiet the excruciating pain. By the time Tom brought the prescription home, the pain had abated and she was resting more comfortably. When bedtime came that evening she willingly crawled into bed and pulled the covers over her body. The pain was much less now and she anticipated a good sound sleep would bring healing during the night. It wasn't long and she began drifting in and out of sleep when the tune *"this ... light.....can't blo..w it ou..t, little ....ligh...t... .,"* softly led her into deep painless sleep.

She would later realize the whispers of the grand Painted Lady was a harbinger of good and not to be feared. In fact she welcomed these whispers of the past. It felt like she was becoming a part of the life of this wonderful home and her own life would become a chapter to whisper in the future.

Several weeks passed and Tricia had put aside the previous experiences of her earlier encounters. She was in the kitchen preparing the dough and baking cookies for a church social. In her eagerness to be helpful she signed up to bring ten dozen and now wondered why she had volunteered for so many. She would be up to her elbows in cookie dough and in the kitchen for most of the morning and part of the afternoon. To help pass the day time, she turned the radio in the living room on to music. She continued mixing the cookie dough, and then shuffled the finished ones from the oven to a cooling rack. She was humming along to I GOT RHYTHM when she heard children's voices coming from the hallway. Thinking her twin granddaughters had slipped in to visit, she called out, "Summer, you and April come into the kitchen and help me with these cookies." She waited for their response and expected them to eagerly come bounding to get their fingers in the cookie dough. When she got no response and the girls did not appear, she wondered if the radio had interspersed some recordings of children. She wiped her hands and went to the living room to change the radio station. Surprisingly, the radio was still loudly broadcasting the song she had been singing.

Confused, she returned to the task of mass cookie making. The radio station finished playing the song and the announcer began his advertising spiel. While taking one batch of cookies from the oven, in addition to hearing giggles and bustling activity behind her, she heard, *"can we have another one?"* No! The radio announcer was promoting laundry soap and the request for 'another one' did not fit the commercial. It took her only a few minutes to make the connection from another time and world. Mrs. Gross, the second lady of the house, made cookies for her children's Bible class. Tricia remembered the children stayed until the last cookie was devoured and they waited for more if she would produce them. At this point Tricia felt she was becoming bonded with this house. It just wasn't a house any more. It was alive with people from the past reassuring the current habitants of the love and purpose that the previous generations enjoyed. The voices Tricia heard were the people anchored by their love of the Lord and telling how this love impacted their lives within these beautiful walls.

Tricia finally finished the cookies, and after a busy day she reached for a glass of iced tea and collapsed onto a kitchen chair. She would definitely share this new experience with Tom when he got home.

As the summer months wore on and the days became longer,

she and Tom decided to have a group of church friends over for an afternoon back yard BBQ. Each couple insisted that they bring a dish to go with the grilled ribs. It became an enormous food fest with the best of each wife's recipe book! A time was set for 2:00 on Saturday. They would meet at the spacious back yard patio located under the giant oak trees. Tricia set out lawn chairs and additional tables. When she finished the patio was a festive scene decorated with colorful pillows and cushions. She was excited to get together with their friends and she quietly prayed the weather would cooperate and not pour rain on the party.

The weather DID cooperate! The day dawned clear and sunny with a slight breeze. One by one the couples arrived and the picnic table groaned with the abundance of food. Tom brought out and set up the croquet game Tricia found at a garage sale a month before. He had also made two horseshoe pits at the very back of the yard. They were ready for an afternoon of fun and food! Several guests were eager to try the croquet game. It had been a long time since they had had the opportunity to play this old fashioned game. The guys chose horseshoes, and some of the gals preferred to sit under the shade trees and visit. The afternoon wore on with the sound of chatting and some voices expressing frustration of missed scores. This was a lively group of people. Happy sounds emanated around the entire back yard. When the players came up for a breather and helped themselves to iced tea and lemonade, several commented on hearing the happy sounds of children playing with a barking dog next door. When they inquired about the family living there Tricia looked surprised and replied, "There is an older couple living next door. There are no children in the neighborhood and certainly no dogs on the block." Some of guests were certain they had heard the laughter of children, and an occasional bark of a large dog. Tricia and Tom didn't have an answer at the moment. They were sure, however, the laughter of children playing was the voices of the Gross family and the barking dog was Hansel. They felt it was best to keep those things to themselves. Beside who would believe them anyway? As the afternoon wore on the guests continued to enjoy the delicious fare. Settled in comfortable chairs they chatted and laughed until the afternoon began to fade into twilight. As they were leaving multiple thanks to Tom and Tricia for a wonderful time echoed through the air.

After all the guests had left, Tom and Tricia collapsed on the glider, pleased the day was nearly perfect. Everyone seemed to enjoy themselves. They didn't speak for a few minutes looking at each other, knowing the thoughts of the other. Others had experienced an episode of the Painted Lady. The past generations had joined in the activities and fun of their party. Truly it was a warm and fuzzy sensation of kinship with the families whom the Lady had kept alive for all these years. Tricia thought she might even write a book relating the fascinating stories of this house.

OPAL'S FARWELL

The summer months were quickly fleeing when Tricia received a letter from Opal asking if she could stop by for a visit on the way to Yellowstone Park. She and Brenda and Chris were on vacation and would like to see her. Tricia was excited at the thought of seeing Opal. She quickly replied telling her how delighted they were to see her. She urged them to spend the night before continuing on to Yellowstone. Opal gave Tricia the date they would arrive, but they could stay only for a short visit because they had confirmed reservations at the Lodge in Yellowstone. If they were delayed their reservations would be canceled and their names would be placed on a long waiting list. Tricia immediately started planning for their visit including baking her favorite pistachio cake.

When Opal and her family arrived Tricia and Tom welcomed them with open arms. It was wonderful to see them all but it was especially great to see Opal. They had been in contact with her several times through correspondence and now they could visit in person. There was so much to share and Tricia was eager to hear about Opal's new life in California. The afternoon was filled with exciting conversations. Tricia interrupted the chatter to serve cake and coffee.

As they lingered over coffee, Tricia began sharing the events they experienced since moving into the house. Opal had a twinkle in her eye as she listened. She smiled and said, "Oh yes, you have been welcomed into the Painted Lady's family." She continued to explain how she had learned and appreciated living with the memories and the voices the walls had shared. It had been a blessing after her husband died and she was left alone with the children. His presence seemed to linger with the spirits of those gone before and it was like having a family comforting her in her loss. To her it was a gift from God reassuring her that she was not alone and she was much loved.

After they left Tricia and Tom lingered over another cup of coffee and began recounting the events that had just transpired. Opal's disclosure was the confirmation that they had become the ongoing family joining those who had lived before. This was a beautiful feeling. They would welcome any future visits knowing God had indeed been in this place.

THE PASSING OF THE LEGACY

Opal sensed her death was near. She sat down one afternoon to write a legacy for Tom and Tricia about her beloved Painted Lady. With Butterscotch curled peacefully in her lap, she began to write. The words flowed from her heart as she wrote:

Tom & Tricia,

I want you to know the Painted Lady as I knew her. She is a real being, you know. Her heart beats with the same emotions of each family residing within her. She remembers each day and stores it away to become a storybook of memories. You can whisper her name knowing she will listen. You will find comfort and joy in her, chasing away cares and concerns. Delight and rest in her presence and she will embrace you with warmth and serenity. Love her and she will guard you with her love. I place her legacy into your safekeeping.

Opal Covington

The grand old home now stood proudly for the world to see. Once again, she WAS the gilded Painted Lady. The morning of a new day burst forth with its brilliant light. Its rays focused on this beautiful lady with her vibrant colors, reflecting her regal status. She once again stood in the spotlight of her history. Her true beauty would come from within her heart as each new family made memories within her walls. There would be whisperings in the night once again, for **'All those who live within my walls will be whom I become.'**

Night Whispers Family Chart
Victorian Painted Lady Named for Beatrice (Bea) Humphreys

Surname	Husband	Wife	Children (by birth order) and their spouses and grandchildren	Time in the House
Humphreys	S.T. (Samuel)	Beatrice (Bea)	Christopher Elliott	1885-88
Gross	Aaron	Johanna	Ernest Albert Jennifer Heidi Rosemary	
			Carol	
			Annette	
			Scottie and unnamed	
Covington	Mike	Opal	Brenda Alice George	
			Chris Austin	
			Unnamed Unnamed	
Johnson	Tom	Tricia	Unnamed	
			Unnamed	
			Summer April	

Homestead Family

Erickson	Unnamed	Unnamed	Dolly Norman Unknown Unknown Unknown Henry	

Pets

Gross Family – Hansel
Brenda and Chris – Butterscotch (BS)